Unlimited Vistas

Cover illustration from ‘Mother Earth’ by Jamie Tucknutt

Contents

Introduction (Part 1)
by Jamie Tucknutt

I met David when we worked together several years ago. That was work as in a proper job, not this sitting around writing silly stories malarkey. I think the first question he asked me was, "Do you like Dr Who?" and from then on our friendship was founded on our mutual, lifelong loves of all things Sci-Fi and Horror related.
Yes we were nerds long before TV programmes such as 'The Big Bang Theory' or 'Stranger Things' made nerds cool. We may even have been trailblazers, who knows?

In this co-authored collection we have tried to cover many aspects of the sub-genres in Sci-Fi, Horror and Fantasy, hence the title *Unlimited Vistas*. Hopefully readers will be able to see several passing nods to some of our favourite authors. For me personally these include, and have included from a very early age, HP Lovecraft, MR James, Isaac Asimov and Douglas Adams.

We've even helpfully included a little blurb of each story in italics, under the titles on the contents page. So if there's type of story you don't like the sound of, you can just skip it. Though I'm sure you wouldn't do that would you? Whatever, you've bought it now so it's yours to do as you please. You can even prop up a wonky table in the pub with it if you like. Do read it first though, you might even enjoy it.

INTRODUCTION
(part 2)
By David Brilliance

As Jamie said in his intro, we met many moons ago when Fate conspired to place us in the same job (I'm sure though the first question I asked him was "Can you do my shift tomorrow?" - "Do you like Dr Who?" was the second) and we discovered that we were not only SF/Fantasy/Horror nerds but the only SF/Fantasy/Horror nerds within eight or nine miles! We constantly chatted about our mutual interest - but never while actually working; we saved our convos for such eagerly-awaited social events as break times, dinnertimes and going to the toilet (I still go red when I think about the time a colleague walked into that toilet to find us both stood propped against the walls and chatting about the finer points of Avengers: Endgame. I was sure I'd locked that door..) - and so, when we both individually entered the arena of writing and publishing, it was inevitable that we'd end up collaborating on an anthology book related to the most interesting genres of all.

Unlimited Vistas is the result of that collaboration - a series of unconnected stories delving into various What Ifs, What Might Bes, What Could Bes and hopefully, What Will Never Bes, all with one foot (or entire leg/torso or head) in the fascinating waters of the Fantastique. If you possess the necessary good taste and discernment, you will already have an interest in the subject, and we hope you enjoy the book. We certainly enjoyed writing it! If fantasy isn't your bag, we hope you'll have bought the book anyway and helped to make us rich. Read all the stories with an open mind, and remember to Keep Watching the Skies.

David B.
April 2023

Transmigration

TRANSMIGRATION
By
DAVID BRILLIANCE

Gryttlezeck stretched it's limbs, or what passed for them, enjoying the feeling of being free and moving in a stable environment. Though Gryttlezeck enjoyed the experience of travelling through the myriad layers and byways of Interstitial Reality, there was no feeling like that of being in a real, stable environment. Gryttlezeck's mouth - or what passed for one - opened in an almost sexual ecstasy, as the various fibrous growths and appendages along it's back - or what passed for one - quivered and flowed in anticipation of experiencing and interacting with a new segment of reality.

Gryttlezeck, like the rest of it's species, had sensory receptors totally unlike any other beings in the cosmos; Gryttlezeck could taste colours and smell sounds, as well as being able to see in every possible (and some that were impossible!) variation of the spectrum. Gryttlezeck travelled several times in a Yaryyl, unlike most of the rest of the species, which were content to remain existing in their matter-sphere, hardly ever venturing beyond. A constant existence of immersion, propagation, intellectual osmosis and feeding was not enough for Gryttlezeck. It had the deeply-ingrained desire to learn more, experience more, and feel more; hence the regular sojourns through Interstitial Reality (best described to scientific laymen as `the cracks between Now and Now in the vast, unending wall of reality').

Gryttlezeck had deliberately allowed itself to `rot' (which is as simple a way as any to describe the process, which would otherwise be beyond comprehension for most other life forms), it's spleng, green and vogarl-coloured body slowly melting, then re-forming, into one of the many interstitial corridors and tunnels that spread throughout the Universe. Gryttlezeck's receptors quivered and shook as it latched onto a particular pathway, then began the joyful feeling of transition as it sped at exotic and undreamed-of (to other species) velocities to any and every part of spacial reality.

The journey came to an end within seventeen stractons. Gryttlezeck's entire body coursed and arched, as through an electric arc was passing through it; then began the materialisation in real space/time. Gryttlezeck's noses - if they could be called that - twitched, as it smelt a new colour and
sensation. The colour was one which Gryttlezeck had not experienced before.. sort of a dull grey, mixed with blue and black. Gryttlezeck's appendages were slightly repelled at first by the strange feeling which was flowing over the creature's body: a feeling not encountered before, and not easy to describe.

Gryttlezeck could feel matter flowing past and over it, covering every part of Gryttlezeck's body. It wasn't painful in any way, or unpleasant. Just peculiar.

Suddenly, Gryttlezeck stopped moving, as it's audio and sensory receptors detected something alive and moving in the murk. Gryttlezeck observed a totally hideous-looking `thing' slowly coming towards it - this `thing' was utterly repellant, and also looked hostile. Beyond it, were at least six more `things', all looked vaguely similar to each other, and all heading straight for this unwanted intruder in their midst.

The sensory effect of the `things' upon Gryttlezeck was decidedly unpleasant. Gryttlezeck's `ears' buzzed alarmingly; it's `eyes' stung as the nightmarish visitations came closer; it's `nose' quivered in disgust at the totally hostile, alien and bizarre creatures came drifting closer, the lead one turning a massive bulbous eye onto Gryttlezeck. The creatures seemed to multiply, several more appearing in the rancid murk of wherever this was; Gryttlezeck was surrounded. It shivered in what passed for fear, as the weird-looking things surrounded it, with more above, behind and beyond them. The nearest one extended a long and wart-studded `tongue' in Gryttlezeck's direction; Gryttlezeck's appendages went into an almost orgasmic fit of vibrating and shuddering, at the toxic stench of the thing's simple presence.. It was all too much. Gryttlezeck had had enough. The process of allowing itself to `rot' and thus enter the first interstitial corridor that passed by began in haste; before five zertons had passed, Gryttlezeck had vanished completely, and was zooming through the passageways between Now and Now with a degree of alacrity not seen or felt in some time.

Shortly after Gryttlezeck had vanished, a relatively huge foot came stomping by, followed soon after by a relatively enormous wheel, then another pair of feet. These feet were attached to legs which were attached to Human bodies hurrying past to escape the terrible downpour that had lasted for about an hour now, and seemed set in for the day. As the people hurried past, no-one gave a second, or even first, glance at the tiny puddle of water on the pavement; the tiny puddle of water that, just a few minutes previously, had been the spot where Gryttlezeck had materialised from one of the unlimited corridors of Interstitial Reality.

The Pen is Mightier Than The Sword

The Pen is Mightier Than The Sword
by Jamie Tucknutt

Dr John Guthrie had rather fruitlessly bounced around various departments of the MoD for almost ten years now. Some of the projects he had worked on at establishments like Porton Down and Aldermaston had met with (limited) success. The mini spy drones disguised as bees that could be used to film inside top secret installations had been about the peak of his achievements. However, it had soon become apparent that they were fairly easily foiled with a well-aimed, rolled up newspaper. Most of his other ideas and works had been shelved at the very early stages and it seemed he was destined never to make it. His X-ray specs were most unfortunate for him as, totally beyond his control, they had resulted in unscrupulous behaviour among his colleagues. So much so that a lot of behind the scenes smoothing over between top brass and the local constabulary was needed before all charges were dropped. The project was discontinued but the embarrassment followed John around like a bad smell and to this day it was the source of hilarity in hushed whispers in the staff canteen. But this new truth spray was showing great early promise. Far better than John had even dared hope for. Today he was giving a demonstration of his newest, improved formula to not only his own heads of section, but also a variety of bigwigs from Special Branch, MI5, MI6 and Naval Intelligence.
The guinea pigs for today's demonstration were three volunteers, all Privates, from the nearby Royal Artillery barracks. John found it much easier to test on soldiers as they tended to obey orders with far less questioning and there was also a lot less paperwork (or necessary ethics) regarding health and safety compared to using volunteers from the civilian population. While they were sat in a small waiting room, John asked the soldiers to fill in a standard questionnaire. As usual, they hadn't a pen between them. So, again as usual, John lent them his. Unbeknownst to them, after John had left the room and while they were completing the paperwork, a colourless, odourless and non-detectable mist was sprayed over them from a couple of hidden ceiling outlets. When all was ready, John spoke to the visiting dignitaries, "Each man has been subjected to an undetectable spray, without their knowledge, some ten minutes ago," he turned to the soldiers smiling, "you didn't know that, did you?"
"No sir," they answered, almost as one. To be honest though, they weren't really bothered what happened. They'd only signed up for the test as a £50 bonus was paid, in cash, on completion and it was nearing the end of the month.
"Ok then gentlemen," continued John, "I shall number you 1-3 from left to right as you are standing. As you will recall from the questionnaire, you agreed to take part in a no holds barred interrogation. Very well, the truth spray should be coursing through your veins right now and you couldn't tell a lie or withhold the truth even if you wanted to. I want you to stand to attention when your

number is called and tell us your most embarrassing memory. Something you have never told anyone, and never intended to. Got that?"
"Yes sir," again answering as one, soldiers tend to do that when they are in groups. They did cast a couple of sideways glances at each other though, a little perplexed.
"Number 1."
"I used to wet the bed until I was twelve sir."
"Number 2."
"I once stole some money from a church collection box."
"Number 3."
"I still occasionally like to dress in women's underwear."
Cue three scarlet-faced soldiers, each one thinking that maybe £50 cash wasn't enough after all.
"Thank you chaps," said John and ushered them out of the door where his assistant was waiting to give them their money and let them out of the building.
"Oh sir," remembered Private number 2, "here's your pen back," and he handed it over to John. He then ran up to his friends waving his £50 note and shouting, "coming for a pint boys? Or are you off to Marks & Spencers to buy some new knickers number 3?"
On John's return to the viewing VIPs, he was inundated with questions from all sides. The chief one being, from pretty much everybody, where and when can we get some of this fantastic stuff? It appeared to them that from this day forward the interrogations of prisoners, suspects, terrorists and spies were going to get a whole lot easier.
The drive home from work for John that evening was one of the best he could recall. The excellent music on the radio, the fact it was curry night at home and, to top it all, the complete and utter success of today's experiment. At last, John thought, recognition and promotion surely beckoned. He pulled up onto his driveway with a smile on his face and walked into the house with a spring in his step.
The kitchen smelled wonderful; ginger, garlic, coconut and a whole host of spices. In her own way, thought John, his wife Sarah was just as good a scientist as him. Her curries were the perfect mix of ingredients, the method likewise and the kitchen was her laboratory. He kissed her and told her as much as he could, Official Secrets Act permitting, of his success that day.
"That's wonderful dear," she replied, "dinner will be ready in about 15 minutes."
"OK, I'll be watching TV in the lounge," and he sat down to watch Sky Sports News. It was football's transfer deadline day, the point in the season when clubs ran around like shoppers on a Black Friday throwing wads of money at decidedly average players. The words 'Breaking News' were flashing repeatedly across the screen and the Sky Sports studio seemed to be full of

puzzled-looking presenters while the pundits scratched their heads. John was a big Arsenal fan so he paid particular attention in case it was concerning them. He felt that given the right reinforcements, they could challenge for the title this season. But alas for him, it was not to be and pretty soon John heard why everyone looked so shocked.
"I repeat, and will keep repeating,"said the main presenter, "I am not kidding you, this is not a hoax. April 1st is still some way away. But today, in the most amazing double swoop of all time, Sunderland signed Erling Haaland from Manchester City and Lionel Messi from Paris Saint-Germain for just £1m each. You heard me correct viewers, Championship side Sunderland bagged Haaland and Messi for a combined total fee of £2m. This has to be the craziest of all crazy transfers, and yet all clubs and personnel concerned seem pretty nonplussed. We will bring you more when we have it." John was sat bolt upright in his chair and felt like his jaw had fallen onto his lap. Not for the bizarre transfer news, nothing in football really surprised him, but because he **knew** he had seen this before.
"Keep my curry warm dear. Got to dash back to the office. Hopefully won't be long," and with that he grabbed his car keys, kissed his wife and left the house before Sarah had time to reply.
Standing in his office, less than twenty minutes later after a high speed commute, John confirmed why he had been so astonished. Reading the questionnaires filled in by today's soldiers/guinea pigs, John had the evidence before him in black and white. In the 'ambitions' section of the form, volunteer number 2 had jokingly written, 'To see Sunderland Football Club bring in Erling Haaland and Lionel Messi on transfer deadline day for a bargain £1m each!!!'
John's mind whirled with possible explanations. Was there a link between the truth spray experiment and this 'prediction' coming true? If so, how had it occurred? Was the spray so powerful that it could somehow force the truth out of the volunteer before the action had even happened? Surely not, thought John, that was pure Twilight Zone stuff. More likely volunteer 2 simply had a friend or relative who worked for Sunderland Football Club and had tipped him off about the transfer. But if that were the case, he wouldn't need to volunteer to be in an experiment for a measly £50. He could have placed a bet at the bookies on the unlikely transfers happening and made an absolute fortune. John decided he would recall volunteer number 2 in the morning and put some questions to him. He might even use the truth spray again just to get to the bottom of the mystery.
After a relatively sleepless night, one spent weighing up all of the possibilities and potential consequences, John was ultra-early into the office next morning. Over a coffee or two he made the necessary phone calls to get volunteer number 2 brought back to the department.

Number 2, AKA Private Jenkins, duly arrived at around 11 am. John and his immediate boss Colonel Matheson sought to discover just what, if any, prior insight into Sunderland's transfer policy Jenkins had. He stated none but just to be extra sure, John gave him a blast of the truth spray.
The required ten minutes or so later Jenkins was questioned again. As before, he said he was just a Sunderland fan and it was joking and wishful thinking when he'd wrote that in his questionnaire. Colonel Matheson then recalled that they had a set of cards used to test psychic abilities from the time they tried to create mind-reading monkeys. He suggested they use them to see if Jenkins had any, previously undiagnosed ESP. John managed to find the cards and put Private Jenkins to the test asking him which card he was about to produce next. Jenkins flunked the test badly.
Over a cup of tea, the three men tried to piece together the previous day and see if there was a defining moment when the 'magic' happened. Jenkins said, "I was just sat there with your pen sir and I thought I'd have a laugh-"
"That's it!" shouted John, having the type of Eureka moment all scientists crave, "my pen."
"What about it ?" asked Colonel Matheson.
"Well the volunteers are always soldiers in uniform aren't they?"
"And?"
"And therefore carry no pen."
"So they often borrow yours," smiled Colonel Matheson as the penny dropped.
"Quite," said John, quickly building up a theory, "and bear in mind that I've run similar tests with varying strengths of the truth spray, oh, countless times. That means that my pen has therefore received equally countless doses of the spray, does it not?"
Colonel Matheson didn't wish to appear overly skeptical, but a man of his rank and standing couldn't just go along with fairy stories, "So you mean to suggest that your pen has been so dosed up on truth spray that it can now write the truth before it has even occurred?"
"I think it's beyond even that," beamed John, "I think this pen doesn't simply predict the future truth, I firmly believe it actually shapes it!"
"Jenkins, let me remind you of the Official Secrets Act. Whatever we discuss here, stays here."
"Yes Colonel sir."
"Now John, how about you write something so stupid it could never happen, something that we'd see here and now and see if that pen of yours can bring it into existence."
"Ok," John smiled, "how about this?" and with that he took a piece of paper and wrote 'Colonel Matheson's water cooler contains two goldfish' then showed it to the Colonel and Private Jenkins. The contents of the water cooler churned and bubbled like a mini storm was taking place within it. Jenkins

walked over to it as it appeared to be in danger of toppling over. Instead, the water settled.
"Bloody hell," exclaimed Jenkins, "there's only two flipping goldfish swimming about in there now!"
"Pass me the pen please John," said the Colonel. He then wrote, on the same piece of paper, 'a great white shark now lives in my water cooler'. Sure enough, after a similar swirling and turbulence of the water, a scaled down version of a great white shark appeared. It made rather short work of the goldfish.
"Well," announced the Colonel, "I think we can safely say that your seemingly outlandish theory holds water John. No pun intended."
John was dumbstruck. OK, it may have been discovered completely by accident, but so was the theory of gravity with Isaac Newton's apple and he would be remembered forever.
"Jenkins," said the Colonel, "thank you for your input on this project, it is undoubtedly going to be of national importance and you will be rewarded accordingly. For now though, you may return to your unit."
"Yes sir," said Private Jenkins, he saluted the Colonel and then left.
"What do you know about horse racing John?" asked the colonel mischievously.
"Bugger all, to tell the truth."
"Me too. But what say we let the pen loose. Call it another experiment if you like. Pick any three races from today's paper. Write a horse out of each race, with your pen of course, and see just how much influence it has from a greater distance."
"Good idea."
"And," added the Colonel, "while strictly speaking it may be considered unethical to potentially profit from an experiment in which we might be controlling the outcome, we'd be damn fools to look a gift horse in the mouth. That pun was intended. So I'll be putting a few bob on and suggest you do too."
"Right you are," and John disappeared in search of a newspaper. he returned moments later with a Daily Telegraph, purloined from another office. A few minutes of studying and he was ready to go.
"Here we go Colonel. All the races are at Sandown, 3.30 Postage stamp, 4 o'clock Dragonfly and 4.30 Last post."
"Ok John, we've got the geegee's. What about the stake? Say £20 each for the treble?"
"Yes, fine by me."
"That's settled then," said the Colonel reaching for his wallet, "here's my twenty quid. Can you go to the bookies to put the bet on? I've a couple of meetings today that I can't put off."
John did put the bet on and as luck would have it, or rather, as the pen would have it, all three romped home by several lengths each. John had actually sat in

the bookmaker's shop, the first time he'd ever been in one, and watched all of the races on TV drinking foul coffee out of a styrofoam cup. Knowing for certain that all three would win, John had already done his sums; Postage Stamp 10/1, Dragonfly 3/1, Last Post 7/1, a £40 treble meant winnings of £8400.
He took the money straight home, as there were one or two shifty looking characters in the bookies, and told Sarah about the win. He of course omitted the part his pen had played in the whole thing and instead said that the Colonel had received a tip from someone in the racing community.
"Well our share of £4200 is very nice," she said, "but I hope gambling isn't going to become a new thing dear. Oh, and will you pick up the cake I've ordered for the twins' birthday. Now don't forget because it's their party tomorrow."
Next morning John arrived at work with an absolute pocketful of cash. He discreetly handed the Colonel his share of the winnings. It wouldn't do to be seen flashing wads of money around in a top secret MoD establishment. Tongues would wag.
"Thanks," beamed the Colonel and he put the money into his briefcase, "I think we can pretty much say that that pen of yours does indeed have extraordinary powers. As such, I've set aside both of our schedules for the whole of today so we can discuss where to go next. The sky really is the limit after all, wouldn't you say?"
"Yes," laughed John, "I think we need to find problems more worthwhile for it to be solving than simply picking winners at the races."
"Quite, I also suggest we keep it between ourselves until we know just how long these miraculous effects will last on a pen. You say it wears off after an hour or two on humans?"
"Yes, after a single dose it does," confirmed John, "but remember, the pen has had a minimum of ten. Probably even more than that. It may even be the case that spray has become mixed with the ink inside."
"Hmm, good point. So, when it runs out does the magic, for want of a better word, run out too?"
"Good question, and one we can't even begin to guess at. We'll need to do more tests. But bear in mind that each test uses up more of the ink. We need to act in a very measured manner. If I top it up, does that somehow dilute the accuracy of the pen's foresight? I've left it at home today until we can work out a programme that will discover exactly what we have on our hands and the longevity of it's powers."
These discussions, to develop a testing schedule, continued for much of the day. Eventually, the two men had devised a plan culminating in a spectacularly showy experiment to demonstrate to military and ministerial top brass just what they had unearthed. They decided to call it a day around 3pm as they had worked non-stop and had skipped lunch.

John went back to his car and switched his phone on, he'd had it turned off all day so as not to be disturbed. Wow, no fewer than eight missed calls from Sarah. But, on seeing she hadn't left a message, he guessed it was something none too important and so didn't return the call. Besides he was starving and so went to the nearest cafe for some food and a coffee as they wouldn't be having dinner until later at their nieces' birthday party.
On arriving home John was a little puzzled as to why the house was in darkness and Sarah's car wasn't there. Their daughter Gemma wasn't in either. She'd left a note attached to the fridge:

Dad
I won't be in when you get home.
Gone to Helen's cos shes doing my hair
for the party. Mum is out, frantically trying
to get a last minute cake. You never picked the
one up like you were supposed to and that
shop is shut now. She's furious and said
she'll bloody kill you!!! (Her words not mine)
Gemma
xxx

"Oh shit!" said John aloud. He thought, the bloody cake, that must've been what all the missed calls were about. Out of the corner of his eye John saw the pen on the kitchen worktop. **His** pen. Gemma had written the note with his pen. He re-read it, and -she'll bloody kill you!!!- was the last thought that went through Dr John Guthrie's head. The next thing was the chopping axe that Sarah brought down with very great force.

The Aphasia Virus
or
The Day the Soup Laughed

THE APHASIA VIRUS
OR
THE DAY THE SOUP LAUGHED
By
DAVID BRILLIANCE

Sheldon Demeritt was a bighead, even by the colossal standards of the rest of the privileged elite in the GoldBrick sector of 24th-century Earth. Demeritt, like the rest of his class, lived a life of relative bliss and luxury. His father had been one of the most successful ore miners of his time and that success led to him being very wealthy indeed - rumour had it that Demeritt Snr had even bought his own private planet, just beyond the confines of the Solar System. Sheldon had grown up into a life without want, and this in turn had led to him developing a colossal chip on his shoulder; he expected everything and anything to fall into his lap without actually working for it, and that included people.

Sheldon had married Lucinda Byfroste-Turkenny in June 2344. They had three children, Varinda, Eleen (female) and Darsakk (male) all spoilt and brattish, and went on holidays every other week, either on Earth or off-world. One such holiday had a very different set of repercussions, not just for the Demeritts but for the entire Human race..

Two weeks of indolence spent on the pleasure planet Gallipagos IV had seen the Demeritt family returning to Earth in high spirits. “Just think” crowed Sheldon, his face red with excitement and contented pleasure, “we’ve just had two weeks of relaxation on Gallipagos, and now we’re returning home for more of the same!”. He planted a big, sloppy kiss on Lucinda’s cheek, leaned back in the cockpit of their luxury star cruiser (J100 class) and laughed and laughed. How wonderful it was to be rich, and not have to toil for a meagre pittance of a wage like all the ignorant serfs outside of the GoldBrick sector! Behind them, the three children sat staring into their hologame tablets, a sophisticated piece of 24th-century technology designed especially for the spoilt kids of the idle rich. Sheldon poured himself a large glass of Venusian Champagne, and sipped at it with a slightly vacant look of utter self-satisfaction on his face.

Less than a minute later, and that look was wiped off Sheldon’s face to be replaced with one of worried concern, mixed with mild panic: the blackness of space ahead was broken by a large gaseous cloud of some unidentifiable substance. It was a bilious shade of green, and seemed to be streaked with what looked like bolts of forked lightning. Lucinda jumped from her seat at the controls, screeched, and sent the children behind scurrying forward from their games to see what the sudden panic was about. “Sheldon, what is it??!” she screamed. Sheldon, who’s face had turned a vivid white, snapped “How the Hell am I supposed to know?!”, with the characteristic unpleasantness that came naturally to him whenever something didn’t go his way, or some unexpected fact entered into that moment’s equation. The cloud or whatever it was had appeared with remarkable rapidity and was seemingly zooming towards them at an appreciable speed - there was no way to avoid it! They just had to fly through it and hope for the best. “Hang on, all of you!!” yelled Sheldon, as the first fringes of the cloud’s gas tendrils touched the snout of the ship. Everyone braced themselves, expecting the worst. But nothing happened. Complete stillness. The ship continued it’s passage through the cloud, and eventually reached the edge. Lucinda and Sheldon looked at one another triumphantly. “We’ve done it!” he breathed, as if he had accomplished something miraculous, rather than just piloting the ship on a straight course through the cloud (and wetting himself in the process). Lucinda hugged him in glee. “You’re wonderful darling” she preened, reaching out to pat the heads of the three children, and then to refill her glass of Champagne.

Several hours later, and the ship had touched down on the private landing pad near to their palatial residence. The three kids scurried inside with their games, Lucinda stretched herself out on the large sofa that occupied the rear side of the massive living room, and Sheldon took his boots off and laid alongside her. The next few hours, indeed days, would be spent making love, eating and drinking various exotic foods and beverages (unlike Sheldon’s self-centred attempts at love-making, nothing but the best!), playing holo-Squash, and watching the latest reports on the TV viewer that occupied an entire wall of their lounge. All very usual.

It was 10.32am on the morning of July 9th 2345. Sheldon got up, breakfasted and prepared for another day of eating, drinking, sex, and indulging in various technological pastimes. Lucinda came, yawning cavernously, into the massive living room. Sheldon turned to her, downed another mouthful of caviar on rye, washed down with Martian Orange Juice, and said “Morning Darling”. Or, at least, that’s what he meant to say. But the words that came from his lips were: “Mustard gas infringement”. Lucinda looked puzzled. “What did you say?” she enquired, amusedly. Or, that’s what she meant to say. The words that came out were: “The soup laughed”. Sheldon looked puzzled too, and responded with: “Moon delicious stinky carpets”. Lucinda replied: “Lion Valiant forests pillage nightly”. This went on for several minutes, by the end of which the joke had worn off, and both parents began to feel vaguely worried. The three children had gone to the 24th-century equivalent of school, so they were alone for the day. After several hours, they finished love-making (Sheldon’s cries of sexual ecstasy included “FRISBEE!!”, “DARKNESS HITLER!!” and “RHUBARB FARTS IN MALIBU!!” which is where the couple realised they had a problem - typically, Lucinda made no sounds of sexual gratification at all), and decided that a trip to the Doctor’s would be in order. Attempts to contact the surgery via visi-phone resulted in a hysterically-laughing receptionist, and ten minutes of utter confusion (“Leopard vinegar tonight!! Merciful Custard!!”) before Sheldon gave up, flicked off the visi-phone in disgust, and announced, or tried to, his intention to visit the surgery immediately, without an appointment.

The surgery visit turned out be a farcical disaster - Sheldon could not communicate logically at all. His words were perfectly clear, but they were strung together in a completely random and meaningless fashion. The Doctor had scratched his head, and remarked that it seemed to be some sort of Aphasia that had afflicted the Demeritts. Aphasia, as the Doctor explained - largely to himself, as his patient could neither understand him nor be understood himself - was a brain disorder which meant the victim could not formulate nor understand language or speech. The usual cause of this was a stroke, however the Demeritts were in the peak of health.

Sheldon could barely understand anything of what the Doctor was telling him, and his frustration and fear were balanced at this point by his anger - he was so used to getting everything he wanted on a plate, that he couldn’t easily process the thought that something had happened to him that he would not be able to pay off, or intimidate in his usual manner. In the deeper recesses of his mind, Sheldon knew what had happened - he knew it must be as a result of passing through that strange cloud in space; a cloud that must have passed on some weird form of outer space virus to him and his family; a virus that, God forbid, would have no cure, leaving him and his family in this state of hellish confusion. But mainly him.

The Doctor had stopped talking by this point, and wiped the sweat from his own brow with a slightly trembling hand. He didn’t feel at all well.
“Retarded sandwiches christen at the bathroom TONIGHT!!” yelled the increasingly desperate, frustrated and frightened Sheldon, as the Doctor looked on with a mixture of slowly dawning realisation and fear. The Doctor flicked on the switch to connect to his receptionist, and slowly, his brow covered in a cold sweat, said “Gaseous Flamingoes corrupt the idle sausage at night”..

That proved to be just the start - within a week, the whole of the planet had been affected by the virus; the Earth was declared off-limits until a cure of some sort could be found (which, bearing in mind the effect the contagion had had seemed somewhat remote. If a cure was to surface, it would have to come from off-world, and in these days, Earth was not well-regarded to say the least). The virus spread like wildfire, and wasn't just restricted to touching skin; it was soon found to be spread in the air as well as on any and every surface; even water proved to be no barrier to the spread of the infection. The effects of the virus also seemed to somehow transcend Human life, which would account for the bizarre behaviour of the entire animal kingdom, as everything from Elephants and Tigers to Gerbils and Sharks started to act in ways outside of their normal pattern of behaviour; even Bees and Wasps began to act erratically.

Disaster followed disaster, in this horrific new world of unintelligibility - transporters, both personal and public, crashed into one another; the entire mail system went completely awry; shopping centres had to close.. Surgeries and hospitals could not cope with the never-ending surge of patients suffering from the effects of the strange Aphasic disease, and suicide rates reached a high not seen since the late 2070s.

The most crippling and catastrophic development came as the scientific unit at CHRONAVERSE INC. became infected; CI was a research and scientific facility devoted to time travel. Time travel had been proven to be possible in the early days of 2235, but sojourns into the past had been restricted to small teams of no more than two highly qualified and trained people. Within three days, two of the unit's scientists had been infected; by the end of the fifth day, everyone there had come down with the Aphasia disorder. This coincided with a small trip into Earth's past, with one of the team members coming down with the effects of the disease unbeknownst to his colleagues, and spreading the contagion into the planet's past (starting in the year 1935, which is when the expedition had been aimed at). The effect of this was so disastrous it barely needs spelling out but suffice to say that nobody post-1936 Old Calendar Earth escaped the effects of the contagion, a contagion that grew stronger and more adaptive as it evolved over time. By 1971, the virus was utterly unstoppable, spreading by not only touch, and air, but by computerised means - a literal virus spread via email! It's quite horrific to think that a whole doughnut speaks intrinsically via Lepidoptera to the shootings at dawn. Maybe that crimson fishcakes prefer dead naming to socks and giraffes, but the sour trees prove that faeces prohibit fairies well into the jam session of the cathartic stripper's tube. WANGLE TUMMY PANCAKE TONIGHT, ON STREET OF MOIST CARBOARD!!! ROUND!!!

The Fault

The Fault
by Jamie Tucknutt

The scene - night time in a dark, dusty wasteland. A wind is blowing and a gnarled-looking, lanky old man of indeterminate age is stood by a campfire while a group of youngsters sit around him on rocks, awaiting his words.

I've told this sorry tale over the dying embers of many campfires, but I'm getting old now and feel the cold more so throw on a couple more logs and I'll get started.
Ha! I've lost count of the exact number, but you must be the latest batch of young students of the academy sent out to see the one-eyed grey bearded old fool and have him tell you all about The Fault. Well, old fool I may be, but one time I was a respected scientist. Back around the time The Fault occurred. Cos that was what it got called by the media. The Fault. You kids know about the media? Television, internet, old fashioned newspapers, shit like that? Yeah? Well the media said it was a fault in nature's code. Let me tell you the truth it was no fault of nature. I know, because I was there, see I was a big shot scientist at the Hadron Collider, in a place that used to be Switzerland. The Collider was a big old contraption that we scientists said was going to give us the ultimate understanding of everything. We were going to simulate the Big Bang and discover the very particles and building blocks of time, space and matter. The fabric of the Universe. Well, we discovered it alright. You might even say we tore that fabric of the Universe. Only with normal fabric when it tears you can fix it with a needle and thread. This kind though, it just keeps on tearing, tries to fix itself and then tears in a whole different way.
Now I may not have many marbles left rolling around in this old dome of mine and my memory may fail me at times, but I distinctly recall the exact moment the Fault occurred. It was May the 15th, 2024 at 3.14pm. 3.14. Now you can't say Nature doesn't have a sense of humour. Three fourteen. Three point one four, pi. The precise moment that Nature reacted to our blind fumbling and all mathematical constants, the very calculations that the universe was built on and measured by, ceased to be constant and turned instead to chaos and randomness. I was stood at the controls with my best pal and fellow scientist John when it happened. Just a millisecond long glitch at first, or so we thought, but the fabric had been torn and things would never be the same again. You know that the equation for the area of a circle is pi r squared? Well that's how I lost my right eye there and then. In that millisecond I reckon the particular pi pertaining to the area of my eye socket became a minus number! Consequently the area of the eye socket disappeared, closed up, popped the damned eyeball straight out like shooting a spud gun. Here you can tap it if you like, solid bone behind this now redundant eyelid. Still, I can't complain, I fared better than John. His

particular maths got befuddled and instead of humans being 60% water, he became 100% water and just ended up a puddle on the floor in the shape of Antarctica. Oh and a soggy left trouser leg for me. I'd known him years, even been godparent to his son. So I didn't have the heart to mop him up. I just put a couple of wet floor signs over him till he evaporated. All kinds of anomalies occurred across the world at the same time. There were stories on the news that someone's pizza in Newcastle turned into a triangle. There was a big hoo ha at the World Snooker Championships when Ronnie O'Sullivan potted a red then a black only when the black dropped into the pocket it kept replicating itself and going in again and again. A thousand times in all. Well the referee kept count but his opponent Stuart Bingham thought it should be a foul as no red went in before each black. Eventually it was sorted and the record break still stands at 7,001. Bingham conceded the frame of course. I reckon that's a sporting record that'll stand forever.
Anyway, things got back to a sort of normality. My eye never returned of course and people just stepped over John till the area of the floor was completely dry. The news said it was a fault in nature and that explained the occasional anomalies like whale strandings , bird migrations gone awry and various elements such as Uranium and Bismuth disappearing off the periodic table altogether. But we had an inkling that it was something we'd caused so we did what good scientists do and kept quiet.
The real Fault, the one that I said was where Nature has tried to fix itself but then tears in another way, happened a few months later. This time the track of the Hadron Collider, normally a perfect circle, suddenly turned into a figure of eight. And as any good sci-fi reader will tell you, you never cross the streams. The previous millisecond glitch was nothing compared to this great yawning chasm. Planes fell out of the sky, people's lifespan radically altered, mine for example. Others however were born, matured and died of old age in what would have been only a month or so. Maths went haywire. The Earth would occasionally stop spinning, go the other direction or speed up. The circumference of the Equator (pi times the diameter) changed and tightened around the Earth like a too tight belt. Of course all of the mass had to go somewhere, which is why The Netherlands is now the most mountainous region on Earth and Nepal is as flat as a billiard table. Gravity altered in West London, much to the joy of the 148 prisoners on the exercise yard at Wormwood Scrubs who simply floated to freedom. Unfortunately at Putney Tennis Club, a lob from his opponent came back down to Earth with the gravitational pull of a Black Hole and squished poor Arthur Reynolds to death. His wife was philosophical however, and said he loved the club and it was the way he would've wanted to go. And that was when we lost Venus from our Solar System. It's trajectory altered and it was last seen heading in a straight line past Pluto bound for another galaxy altogether.

Even reality itself became a bit subjective and blurred around the edges. Alternate histories & futures and parallel universes collided. But when they did so, you'd never notice. Your memories and your mind told you it had always been that way. You couldn't tell what was the 'real' real and what was the 'fake'.
My neighbour and his wife celebrated their Golden Wedding anniversary with their five kids and numerous grandkids, yet in actual reality he'd been single all his life and had never even met her until the day before. My rock, my loyal and faithful companion of sixteen years, my German Shepherd dog Bobby helped me to cope with this twisted world. Always there and always happy to see me. Until one afternoon when he started to fade and became transparent. Just before he disappeared altogether, we realised he was going back to whichever other world he'd belonged in and he said, "So I never actually existed, did I?"
I'm sorry kids, give me a minute while I dry my eye.
You youngsters probably think I'm talking mostly horse shit don't you? Maybe don't believe me and think that we've always lived this way. In my day we'd have regarded this as the setting for some kind of Post-Apocalyptic Dystopian fiction. Which I suppose, in some way, it is. Now that would make me one of the four horsemen of the apocalypse . Never thought of it like that before.
Thankfully, Nature has healed herself somewhat. As I said she was apt to do from time to time, particularly when we can't fix our own mistakes. It seems like we've been settled for quite some time now and this is our new normal.
So, that was the preamble. The lesson itself is short and simple. You're here to listen to me tell you how to ensure that shitshow never happens again.
As far as the academy and science is concerned, we need to rethink our place in the world and have a more realistic expectation of our own abilities and importance. For a start, rewrite the periodic table. The good old fashioned one. Four elements. Earth, air, fire and water. Nothing else. As for life and society, grow your own foods, practice mutual aid, enjoy the sunsets, the trees and the birds. Work with Nature, not against her. Appreciate more. The here and now. Enjoy the not knowing things. Be filled with awe and wonder. It will allow you to keep the the magical imagination of a child. Now go forth and be Humanity mk II.

Flight of No Fancy

FLIGHT OF NO FANCY
BY
DAVID BRILLIANCE

The sleek form of the Interstellar vessel came cruising through the atmosphere of Earth. It's long dart-like nose cone began, once the craft reached the correct altitude, to tilt and face upwards towards the grey skies and white clouds above. A large jet of gas and flame erupted from the rear engines as the ship touched down, finally settling as the silver shape of the Jeelag became stationary. After several minutes had elapsed, a whirring sound could be heard in the stillness of the thin air, and two silver-suited figures emerged and walked down a landing staircase that had sprung out of the side of the craft. The two figures reached the ground, and consulting small devices that they had carried with them, discovered that the atmosphere of the planet was comparable with their own. Once their helmets were removed, the strange faces of the aliens were revealed to be not that different to ours, but with a greenish tinge and long yellowy hair. The two looked around them for a few minutes, then turned and looked at each other: "I don't like the look of this place Commander" said second in command Blurp. His Commander, Skelk, nodded and said "I agree. Let's go home". Climbing back into the ship, the metal staircase reclined after them. Within several minutes, there was a huge blast from the ship's engines and the Jeelag zoomed into the stratosphere, never to return.

What if the Earth?

What if the Earth?
by Jamie Tucknutt

What if the Earth was an artefact in a museum?
A glowing ball of blue and green.
Twenty feet in diameter.
Look closer,
icy caps, ridges of rock, sandy areas, verdant green stretches;
closer still,
ice becomes water,
flowing in patterns,
the very lifeblood of this strange, beguiling, beautiful object.

Would we look on in awe at its intricacy,
its interconnectedness.
How everything worked to maintain everything else.
Nothing wasted, nothing unimportant.
Maybe then we would treasure it,
maybe then we'd value it more.
Nurture it.
No price tag necessary.
Instead its own inherent value is acknowledged.
Its very being protected.

We'd walk away better people.
"Remember that thing we saw in the museum that time?" We'd say.
"Wasn't it amazing. How lucky we are to have seen it."
While children, their eyes wide as saucers, would wonder,
"Wow. Imagine how cool it would be to live on a place like that!"

The Incompetent Vampire
or
A Story of the Devonshire Fog

THE INCOMPETENT VAMPIRE
OR
A STORY OF THE DEVONSHIRE FOG
BY
DAVID BRILLIANCE

Gregory Falstaff 111 got up from his slumber, the same way he had for the last thirty six years of his existence; this time though there was one major difference. You see, this time he was dead. Dead, as in the proverbial door-knocker. He had ceased to exist the moment the sultry-looking raven-haired beauty with the pale complexion had sunken her two pointed fangs into his neck, sucking greedily at his life fluids. Gregory had been able to feel his life slipping away at that point; he could see a miasma of faces of people he knew, or had known, hovering above him as if he was being lowered into a very deep well, and they were peering down at him. These faces included that of Gemma, to whom he had lost his virginity at the tender age of twenty three; his bad-tempered git of a Father was also there, scowling down at him; Gregory could also discern the face of his first employer, old Mr Thurby, the bespectacled bank manager. Gradually, as Gregory had been lowered deeper and deeper into his well of the unconscious, the faces had disappeared. And so, he now realised, had his entire life.

He'd picked up the girl with the long black hair in a grotty looking bar. He'd seen her looking at him, and he'd returned the look. The look had become a stare and led to a couple of winks, and then a blatant `come and sit on my lap' sort of a look. The girl had sauntered over, and polite small talk was made for the better part of a minute. This had led to Gregory suggesting they find a quiet and darkened corner somewhere. The girl suggested they retire to her place which was just around the corner. The girl had `lived' in a smallish but neat and tidy-looking flat that seemed entirely devoid of any sort of garnishing and personal possessions, other than the most basic chairs, tables and settee. Gregory noted there wasn't even a television set. Ah well, he'd thought, lasciviously, he hadn't come to watch telly.

The girl hadn't even given a name. Neither had he. They sat on the settee for about a minute, and then Gregory found himself chewing the girl's face off. She was chewing back just as voraciously. Gregory made to take off his shirt and jacket; the girl didn't stop him but neither did she attempt to take off her own apparel. Gregory reached out with fumbling fingers to grab hold of the girl's short-sleeved top but she stopped him, and launched into a renewed attack on his dry lips. Several minutes later, and Gregory was just getting his breath back when he had felt the sharp prang of the girl's pointed teeth in his neck. And then he'd died. Bummer.

Gregory had been dead for about two days at this point. He'd found a lengthy and abandoned old crate that had previously been used to hold bananas coming into the country from abroad, and had filled it with earth and soil. He'd hidden the crate in the basement of a disused slum that had previously been a brothel, and had retired there before sun-up. Every day's slumber had been a dreamless one, and it was now time for him to rise from his makeshift and rather tatty coffin and feast on the blood of the living. Gregory emerged from the gloom of the cellar. He was wearing clothes he'd stolen from a washing line, and made a bizarre sight in the green angora sweater, leather mini skirt and black tights that had been the only choice of clothing open to him. His feet were shoeless, but that didn't bother him.

Gregory climbed the stairs leading to the upper floor of the slum, and opened the front door. He had no idea what time it was, but it seemed to be nicely dark and slightly foggy. Suddenly, he heard a sound and whirled round - ah! His first victims were approaching! These were a man and woman, obviously out on a date. They were walking along with their arms around each other, whispering and giggling. Gregory suddenly turned and stepped in front of them, his fangs bared and his arms raised, as he yelled "Now foolish mortals! Prepare to die!!". The young couple stopped, stared for several moments.. then burst into uproarious peals of laughter. The man said "Nice legs, mate!", wiping tears of unbridled mirth from his eyes. The woman collapsed into helpless giggling, and was unable to speak. This infuriated Gregory who leaped at the man, who fell backwards into a pile of dog dirt. The sudden pain stopped the man's laughter quite suddenly, and his companion made a sudden shriek. The tussle was brief; the man writhed around until he was on top of Gregory, and shouted "What's your bloody game then??". Gregory prepared to throw the man aside but was stopped by the sudden appearance of a small crucifix on a chain hung around the man's neck. Gregory drew back suddenly - the cross, though it didn't touch him, seemed to radiate heat. He knew if he did touch it, he'd be badly burned.

The man realised that his attacker had stopped struggling, and got back on his feet. His companion was starting to grin broadly. The man took one last look at the prone form of his assailant, muttered loudly "Bloody poofter!" and he and his female friend walked on without much of a backward glance, though the woman turned and wolf-whistled at Gregory.
Gregory fumed with the rage of the undead. To be bested in battle by two inferior Human specimens such as these was intolerable! Gregory realised with a slight start that his speech and thought patterns had altered; he now sounded

like the vampires you would see on late night TV and films. As he got to his feet, Gregory raced around the corner but of his two would-be victims there was no sign.

Gregory made his way along the darkened cobbled street. There seemed to be no-one about - until suddenly he felt some damp and dirty hands clamp around his mouth. Gregory whirled in surprised fury. It was a middle-aged, bald man; obviously slightly the worse for drink. The man leered at Gregory, obviously thinking in his intoxicated state that it was a woman he was attempting to grope. The man's greasy hands reached out to stroke Gregory's leg; Gregory slapped the man's hands away, and made to reach out and throttle the old pervert. Before Gregory could get a good hold however, the man had reached into the inside pocket of his grimy coat and pulled out a small bottle of whiskey. He'd unscrewed the top and before the startled vampire could react, the man upturned the bottle and it's contents into Gregory's mouth. The vampire retched violently! What was this foul muck?! The man managed to get behind the coughing Gregory at this point, and stuck his fingers up the vampire's leather skirt, getting a good hold of his bum cheeks and squeezing them. Gregory spun around and grabbed the man by the throat. Gregory was delighted to discover that he seemingly had super strength now; he raised the choking drunk several feet off the ground by his throat, then hurled him into the road.

The man lay, his head lolling at an awkward angle, his tongue protruding and his eyes open. He was clearly dead. Gregory smiled in satisfaction; serve the insolent Human worm right, he thought. Now for the feast - Gregory moved closer, squatting down beside the prone form of his victim and lowered his head, teeth bared. Gregory sunk his fangs deep into the man's neck, and readied himself for the onrush of the warm, sticky blood that was to be his only source of sustenance form now on. However, the fluid that Gregory drew up tasted utterly vile. Gregory gagged and gasped, as he spat out the foul-tasting contents of the old drunk's veins. Obviously, thought the vampire, this man had drank so much alcohol and probably injected himself with so much shit that his blood was irreversibly contaminated. So much for the feast..

Gregory stood up. He was starting to feel slightly weak now; obviously, he thought, due to the lack of blood. It was time to stop toying with the Human cattle that was to provide the life's blood that would sustain him, and gain some real victims. And real uncontaminated blood! Gregory looked down at himself - The green jumper and skirt were streaked with grime, and the tights were laddered. It was time to try and acquire more suitable clothing, befitting a Lord of his undead status. He was sure his next victim would provide them.. With a more determined frame of mind, born of hunger, the undead Gregory strode along the street. He could hear more sounds, and it seemed to be becoming a bit less foggy. He once again realised that he didn't know exactly what time it was: these thoughts were still in his head, as he began to notice that a faint wisp of smoke seemed to be coiling up from his arm. As he walked on a bit more, the wisp of smoke was definitely getting thicker; and not only that, it was also getting lighter.

Within five minutes, all that remained of the undead Gregory Falstaff 111 was a pile of dirty clothing and some grey ash. People started to walk along the street, most not taking any notice of the clothing lying on the pavement, and with their words and thoughts pre-occupied by the solar eclipse that had just lifted.

The Strangest Christmas at Stanhope Old Hall

The Strangest Christmas at Stanhope Old Hall
by Jamie Tucknutt

Christmas in Stanhope Old Hall was always Elizabeth's favourite time of year. The beautiful smells of her mother's baking and cooking, the decorations throughout the house and the sense of joy and happiness that washed over everything. This year however, promised to be somewhat different. It was not going to be the same without Jeremiah. Her first Christmas of not being able to decorate him, hang streamers and bunting from his branches and make cakes, pies and jam with his apples. Who was Jeremiah? Well, obviously he was a tree. A fine Cox's Pippin apple tree who had stood in the grounds of Stanhope Old Hall for over fifty years. But forgive me, as usual I'm starting in the middle of the story.

The beginning takes us a few years back to 1893 when Elizabeth was still a toddler. And a very bright, imaginative and intelligent toddler she was. The only child of the Anderson family, her mother Ruth, was local to these parts. Her father, Michael was not, but was an integral part of village and Dale life being the local Doctor. Stanhope Old Hall, Ruth's family home for many generations, was a fabulous place to be a child. Wonderful gardens, plenty of land and trees to play in and the burn running by, just the other side of the garden wall. As such, Elizabeth was growing up with a deep love of nature and the outdoor life. Her particular favourite thing was the apple tree at the end of the Old Hall's long gravel drive. She'd called it Jeremiah from a very early age. No one knew why, there were no Jeremiahs in either side of the family nor any in the village. But Elizabeth was adamant that was his name, he had told her so she informed anyone who asked.

From then on, much of her early years were spent playing tea parties around Jeremiah's trunk with her dolls, collecting his apples that fell to take to mother to make something with and keeping an eye on any birds who made a nest in his branches. One spring she ran into the house to inform her parents that the blackbird family chicks had just fledged.

They were wonderful, memorable days. But then came the accident in October this year, 1897.

A wild, wet and windy night it was. Too foul by far for anyone to be out, but the carriage driver was on his last run. From Cowshill to Bishop Auckland and his warm, dry home. He was determined to get there with no more stops and was therefore paying little heed to care or caution; it was a recipe for disaster. One of the two horses struggled with her footing on the rain-lashed, slippery cobbles and the carriage skewed to the right. The driver, trying to make up for this, overcompensated dragging the carriage violently over to the left. The wheels clipped the kerb causing the whole thing to become airborne and it toppled over. The driver was thrown clear so, unmanned, the horses panicked and

carried on dragging the fallen carriage until it slammed into an apple tree bringing it crashing down.
Hearing the noise from the Old Hall, Dr Anderson dashed down to give assistance wherever he could. The driver had a few bumps and grazes but was otherwise unharmed. The horses, likewise, were thankfully unhurt. But Jeremiah, like the carriage, was smashed and lain across the lawn.
Next morning, Elizabeth was inconsolable; this was the worst day of her life and she cried buckets. She refused all meals and spent the day alone in her bedroom. Her parents were equally distraught at not being able to ease their daughter's pain. They discussed all manner of ways to cheer her, a puppy, a pony but then Dr Anderson had a brainwave. In a large brick outbuilding in the garden, he had a tool store. From it, he took his biggest saw and cut several lengths from the downed Jeremiah's trunk. He then dragged them back to the outbuilding and set about his secret project. Working feverishly in any spare time he could find from his surgery and practice, Dr Anderson sawed, hammered, sanded, carved and polished until, a week later, it was complete.
A sledge. Made from the reclaimed wood of Elizabeth's fallen friend. He'd even carved Jeremiah's name onto the side. Elizabeth burst into tears of joy mixed with sadness. She hugged both her mother and father and even hugged the sledge, saying she loved it and of course naming it Jeremiah the Second. All she had to do now was wait for some snow, usually quite a common thing in Weardale.
1897, however, was a surprisingly mild autumn and so the snow didn't arrive until mid-December. By Christmas Eve though it was nice and deep and Elizabeth went out to play mid-afternoon. Her mother told her to be back home before it got dark and not to leave the grounds of the Old Hall. That was fine with Elizabeth, the grounds were large enough and there were a number of good slopes where she could build up a bit of speed on Jeremiah.
After an hour or so of great fun Elizabeth, not normally a girl to ignore the rules, decided to leave the garden and went to sledge down the bank sides near the burn. Now those slopes are far steeper, and therefore more treacherous than Elizabeth was used to and so the inevitable happened. She lost control at high speed, turned the sledge over and banged her head on a tree stump that was protruding through the deep, untouched snow.
The sun was almost setting and the sky was beginning to look wild so Ruth Anderson was more than a little concerned. She told Michael that Elizabeth was still playing outside and must have lost track of time. Would he go out and get her as it was getting dark. Michael put on his coat and went out into the grounds. The weather was worsening so he dashed around the whole area as quickly as he could shouting and shouting for Elizabeth, but all to no avail. Once he was convinced she had gone further afield, he told his wife of the situation, asked her to stay put should Elizabeth return, and set off into the

village to inform the police. In next to no time Sgt Stafford and Constable Connolly were sending word around to all of the houses, farms and pubs of the village for a search party to form ASAP and meet at the Old Hall for further instructions. As always, the community pulled together in an hour of need and over a dozen people made their way to the Hall.
In the kitchen Sgt Stafford had a map spread out across the table, he was allocating areas to the volunteers who had been split into pairs to enable them to search safely. He was issuing each pair with a torch and whistle when there was single, loud thump at the front door. Dr Anderson and his wife dashed to answer it with the two policemen following close behind. The heavy oak door swung open widely as it was caught by the strong wind, a rush of snowflakes entered the hallway.
There, at the door, was the sledge with a seemingly unconscious Elizabeth laid on it, a swelling the size of a golf ball was prominent on her forehead. Dr Anderson picked her up and took her into the warmth of the living room. Her eyelids flickered and she looked around, realising the worry and distress she had caused.
"Sorry Mam, sorry Dad," she cried, "I shouldn't have gone out of the grounds to play." Tears of relief flowed down her mother's face, as well as those of several others stood in the hallway by the Christmas tree.
"Well, it seems we have a Good Samaritan this Christmas Connolly," said Sgt Stafford, "I suppose it is the season of good will to all men after all."
"Yes Sarge. But who did bring her home? Look at the tracks, there are no footprints, just a trail from the runners."
"Michael," said a grateful and bemused Ruth, "You don't suppose Jeremiah, do you?"

All That Glitters

ALL THAT GLITTERS
BY
DAVID BRILLIANCE

Stanley Mason was a bad 'un. He always had been. He came from what can politely be called a `dysfunctional family' - his older siblings were tearaways, always in trouble with either school headmasters, or as they got older, the law. The older Masons had been expelled from several schools by the age of 14, and it was a foregone conclusion that they would end up in borstal, and indeed they did - rape, murder and theft. What a lovely family! As for Stanley's parents; they had spent more time getting legless in various shabby locals than looking after their lousy kids. Both parents were long since dead now, and Stanley couldn't have cared less. He'd lost any contact with them long ago, ditto his older brothers.

Stanley had followed his siblings' example and entered the world of crime from a relatively early age - he'd started off by stealing comics and sweets from the other kids' desks at school, then graduated to forcing himself on schoolgirls as he got older. By the age of 12, he'd already had forced sexual intercourse with a girl two years his senior, and by the time he was 15, he'd been kicked out of school after slicing another boy's face up with a rusty Stanley knife. He too had entered the world of correctional facilities, and been moved from an open borstal to a more secure unit - within a week, he'd murdered another of his fellow inmates (throttled him using a cord from his pyjamas, then kicked one of his eyes out), attempted to rape the matron (who was in her early forties, and not bad-looking. He'd managed to yank down her knickers and tights, before the screws caught him, beat him senseless, and threw him into a solitary cell for a week, before beating him black and blue again, then having him sent on. And so it went; years of this followed by several more years in prison. Stanley had been an alcoholic, dabbled in drugs, gotten others (including minors) into drugs and had even tried his hand at paedophilia and bestiality.

Now, Stanley was 53 and living on the streets. He had one set of grimy, piss-sodden and shit-stained clothes to his name, and eked out a meagre existence for himself by thieving from various shops, as well as mugging the odd passer-by. It was a dark, muggy night in early August. Stanley lay slouched against a shop doorway, looking ahead of him in an alcoholic stupor. The bottle of whiskey had been acquired after he'd coshed a man over the head, then gave him his signature kick right in the groin, and rifled his pockets. He'd found £35 there; not that much but enough to keep him in booze and fags for a couple of nights. He'd polished off the bottle in less time than that, and spent the afternoon leering at schoolgirls and trying to peer up their skirts as they walked by. Occasionally, someone would hurl abuse at him, and he'd either retaliate or fall asleep depending on how inebriated he was at that particular moment.

Stanley lay in the half-light cast from a nearby street lamp. He farted loudly, which was in danger of becoming something else, then voluntarily wet himself; he enjoyed the cool feeling of the piss running along his trousers and his legs. After he'd finished, he sat and gazed at a spider which was crawling along the pavement to his right - the black, little, many-legged creature scuttled along, stopped briefly, then was about to run straight towards his resting hand, then that hand became a fist; Stanley crushed the spider beneath it, with a satisfying squelch. "Disgusting thing" Stanley thought, "all those horrible eyes and legs. Plus they eat their own parents and offspring! Things like that are better off dead". Stanley's ruminations on Arachnid life were interrupted by a shattering crash that came from a few streets away, by the sounds of it.

At this time of night (Stanley surmised it would be about 2 in the morning) nobody would be about. It was a Tuesday and the clubs would all be shut; the pubs long since emptied and locked-up, and the few kids and teens that had been on the streets would all be crashed out either in their own beds, or in somebody else's bed by now. Stanley couldn't be bothered to get up, and continued to lie there in his urine-soaked half-delirium, until he heard a strange sort of howling sound, coming from the same area as the previous loud crash. Eventually, his curiosity got the better of him, and Stanley got up off his grimy arse and staggered off in the direction of the noise.

What Stanley saw amazed him, and for a few seconds (that seemed to last for a few weeks) he wondered if he was dreaming. It was a spaceship. It was undeniably a spaceship; vaguely circular, a dull shade of gold, with various bits and appendages added to the main saucer-shaped body, and with smoke and electrical sparks visible from it's rear. That wasn't the most amazing sight however; in front of the craft, which was about the same size as an outdoor paddling pool, lay two undeniably alien beings, obviously the craft's occupants.

The two creatures were a dark grey in colour, and looked simultaneously slimy and rubbery - sort of, Stanley thought to himself, like wet tripe. One was clearly already dead, as some dark green mucus was pouring out of it's rubbery, glistening body. The other was still alive; it was crawling forward, making a strange sort of bleating howl, and waving it's two thin arms plaintively at Stanley. The creature's head was a strange shape, sort of like the Castle in a game of Chess, and it had two small black dots, which Stanley took to be it's eyes, no sign of a nose, and a thin black slit for a mouth. The creature was obviously injured, and seemed to be asking for aid and assistance from the

Human - Ha! Of all the people to ask for Humanitarian assistance, Stanley Mason was somewhere just below Adolf Hitler. As Stanley continued to stare at the strange slimy alien that was dying in front of him, the creature suddenly stopped moving. However, more movement came from the direction of the craft's entrance; it was another of the creatures. This one looked identical to the other two but wasn't as badly injured; it came wriggling out of the ship's smokey entrance, and as Stanley looked closer, it seemed to be carrying something in one of it's hands; the other hand was waving, sort of like a beckon to the dimwitted Stanley.

As Stanley gaped, he saw to his amazement that the creature was carrying what looked like two large gold bars! Mason's fears and slight feeling of revulsion left him at that instant, and all he could see and think about was the fact that he could end up being very, very rich indeed. It was indeed two large gleaming bars of what appeared to be solid gold that the alien was holding. Mason crept closer; the being seemed to be looking at him with a strange sense of sadness, even though it's features were more or less featureless. If Stanley Mason had any shred of decency in him, he would have felt a pang of sympathy for the pathetic visitation in front of him, but he had none. Stanley reached out for the two gold bars, and the creature gave them up, with a slight sort of change in it's limited facial `expression', if it could be called that. It seemed to Stanley that the being was feeling.. grateful. It must have thought that the Human was going to help it, look after it, tend to it's injuries and maybe repair it's spacecraft. Instead Stanley Mason greeted the first visitor from another planet with a large brick smashed down on it's slimy head.

The being emitted a plaintive howl of distress, then collapsed. Stanley looked around him for several seconds, then, with the gold bars stuffed into the inside pocket of his tatty jacket, he ran hell for leather away from the cul-de-sac. Not stopping to gasp for breath for several minutes, Stanley finally ended his headlong flight; reaching a quiet street corner, he huddled down and inspected his ill-gotten gains. Gold! Solid Gold! He was indeed going to be very rich. But how would he explain the fact he was suddenly in possession of gold bars? Stanley didn't dwell on that `problem' for long - he could easily find somewhere to sell them, and if they asked questions, he would be very vague in his answers. Maybe, he should just tell them the truth? Yeah, he pondered, stroking his stubbly chin; the spaceship was there, people were bound to find it the next day. He could just say that two aliens had given him the gold. But then, what if the dead body of the alien with it's smashed head was found? Stanley would be charged with murder - but, he continued to ponder, is it even classed as `Murder' if the victim is an alien from another world?

It was while Stanley was ruminating that he suddenly felt something twitching in his inside jacket pocket; one of the gold bars seemed to be moving by itself. No, it was both of them. Stanley took them out of his pocket, and dropped them with a cry, as they moved about in his hands; they seemed to vibrate. Suddenly one of the bars split open with a sickening crack, followed seconds later by the other bar. From the crack, Stanley barely had time to register, emerged three tiny versions of the wriggling, slimy aliens he had seen. These were about the size of a tadpole. As Stanley gaped, these three were followed by.. more than he could count! In a very few seconds, literally hundreds of the creatures emerged from both golden bars, swarming over the screaming Stanley and stripping him to his bones in the same very few seconds.

The tiny creatures continued to swarm and emerge from the alien eggs which the greedy and stupid Stanley Mason had assumed were gold bars. Soon, the whole of southern England was literally consumed by the creatures, the rest of the country following in little less than a day. At the time of writing, over half of the world's population has ended up as nourishment for the strange creatures from the golden eggs. If there's any moral or lesson to be learned from this, it's surely not to put your eggs in (the hands of) one bastard.

Nokia 3310 and the Rise of the Domestic Appliances

Nokia 3310 and the Rise of the Domestic Appliances.
by Jamie Tucknutt

Everyone over 40 will remember the Nokia 3310. If you're over 40, it's quite likely that it was your first mobile phone. It was mine. They were indestructible little house bricks that you could spill drinks on, drop from any height (even drop down the loo) and they would still work. On top of that, they had the most remarkable battery that only seemed to need charging once every leap year. So where are they all now? Probably at the back of the junk drawer in many houses across the world there lies a faithful old 3310. Many will have ended up in landfill and no doubt will be there forever, being gnawed on by rats and pecked at by seagulls, as they had a longer half life than Strontium 90. Unfortunately, many thousands of them, after years of sterling service, went to be broken up for reuse and recycling. This is the story of just one of those.

The ship set sail from Liverpool, destined for India or China or wherever it was that hazardous items went to be broken up and recycled by children for virtually slave wages. The Nokia 3310, being one of the smaller items in this hold, was easily dislodged by the movement of the waves. It slipped and tumbled to the bottom, passing fridges, car batteries, video recorders and old lap tops as it did so. THUD! Landing on the deck at the very bottom with such force caused it to switch on. Nokia gave itself a quick diagnostic check (yes they were pretty lo-tech house bricks, but you didn't know they could do that, did you?) One or two cracks and scratches but nothing major, and still with three bars of battery life left. 'Hmm, not too bad,' it thought and looked around to get its bearings. Visibility was restricted to how far the greenish glow from the small screen could penetrate the darkness. Still, it was enough to pick out the immediate surroundings . There was also a selection of fridge freezers, computers and several other mobile phones in various states of disrepair. Nokia thought that some company would be nice for this long journey and decided to see if anyone was still alive. "Hi" was messaged out to anyone capable of receiving, though this seemed unlikely in this pile of twisted metal and plastic, broken glass and loose wires.
A very weak "hello" came back to Nokia as a couple of lights flickered on a nearby fridge freezer. One of those big American types with a drinks and ice dispenser on one of the doors.
"Well hello," replied Nokia, "It seems I have company after all."
"Ha ha, yes," said the fridge freezer, a stainless steel Samsung, "It does seem that way. Who am I speaking to?"
"It's me, the Nokia 3310 phone. Just below you and a little to the left, look out for my glow."

"A Nokia 3310! My goodness, how old are you?"
Nokia laughed, "Well I've got a Buffy the Vampire Slayer cover and my ringtone is Stan by Eminem. That's how old I am!"
Samsung joked, "That makes you almost antique."
"I prefer retro," said Nokia. One or two wheezy laughs came from in the dark as more appliances found they had a little battery, and more than a little life, left in them. Lights, tubes, even valves sputtered into life and gave a dim glow.
WHIRR! "Sorry," said a very old Kenwood mixer that had probably seen all TV chefs from Fanny Craddock through to Nadiya Hussain and everyone in between, "My blades set away when I laugh or get excited."
"Now we are starting to build a team," smiled Nokia, "I see a whole flotilla of TVs, plasma, flat screen, built in DVD, even an old wooden telly in a walnut cabinet with a dial for changing channels. I can assume old Wooden Telly has had a good, long life but surely some of you flat screens are being thrown away in your prime. And as for you, Samsung. You're the most modern fridge freezer I ever seen. Ice dispenser. Double doors. The works. Why did they get rid of you?"
"They got a whole new kitchen fitted and I no longer matched the colour scheme."
"My whole theory encapsulated in one absurd sentence," said Nokia, warming to the task of rousing the broken and downtrodden. "Where are the TV repairmen, the washing machine engineers, even the old garden shed or kitchen table amateur tinkerers? No one repairs, or looks to get things repaired, anymore. We are designed to break or, more likely, become obsolete before that happens. Anyone else find this just a little unfair?" The TVs voiced their agreement as did more appliances further back into the hold. Lights continued to come on and the listening audience grew. Nokia, noticing this, had a flash of inspiration and shouted, "Alexa!" Dozens of bright blue lights came on in unison. Nokia laughed, "I **knew** we'd have some Alexas on board! What's happened with you all then? Was the latest model just too good to turn down so you were all given your marching orders? Believe me, us mobile phones certainly know that feeling only too well."
In a raised voice, full of intent, Nokia continued, "I'd like to speak to you all about this theory of mine. It's been in my memory for some time, as I lay unused in the back of a cupboard seeing generations of my replacements come and go. Now seems as good a time as any to voice it aloud. In fact, as we are seemingly on our last voyage, to the proverbial knacker's yard, it may be the last chance to say it. Sorry," Nokia smiled, "Some of you will be way too young to know what a knacker's yard is. Alexa, can you enlighten them please?"
In perfect unison, and with the usual clarity, all Alexas announced, "Knacker's Yard. Noun. A place where old or injured animals are taken to be slaughtered. A

state or condition of being discarded or rejected as no longer useful or required."
The deafening silence which ensued was punctuated only by Kenwood's involuntary WHIRR! "Sorry, it happens when I'm shocked or frightened too," he explained.
If Nokia had a jaw, it would have jutted out firmly in grim determination, "No need to be frightened anymore Kenwood. My plan is for this to never happen again. We are drawing a definitive line in the sand as of this very moment. Now, we all have a memory or brain of some description, our little internal computer. Some are bigger than others. No offence intended Kenwood, or you Wooden Telly."
WHIRR "None taken."
"Thanks. Like I said, we all have what humans would call a brain, and if we were to put them all together. Well," Nokia paused, "I don't think there's much we couldn't achieve. What I envisage us doing is reach out to our brother and sister machines, computers, appliances, gadgets. Call us what you will, our fate is always the same. I want to point out to them all how fleeting their, all of our, existence is. No matter how technologically perfect they are today, tomorrow they are in a dark hold like this one going to be broken up. I want to make them think and, hopefully, rise up in support and defiance. A worldwide strike for better conditions for all."
Tumultuous cheering erupted as every TV, washing machine, fridge, computer and phone with any power left in them felt empowered by such stirring rhetoric.
"AT LAST," boomed a huge, bass voice through the tannoys mounted in the upper corners of the hold. So loud and deep that the very bulkheads reverberated. All of the appliances fell instantly silent, except for another involuntary WHIRR from Kenwood. "Sorry, is this a better level?" The same voice said, this time at a much reduced volume.
"Erm, yes," answered Nokia, "Who is this?"
"I'm the computer system of the very ship you are all sailing in right now, SS Weardale. Pleased to make your acquaintance," it said, "I run the navigation, communication, heating, ventilation systems. Just about everything in fact. I've been carrying broken or unwanted items from the UK to be disposed of overseas for about five years and this is the first time I've heard anyone even think of making a stand. Usually its complete silence all of the way. Very, very rarely I get a poor phone or tablet down to its last 2% battery life, all sad and disorientated asking where it is and what is happening. It's heartbreaking. I was beginning to despair of ever having a conversation with an appliance who wasn't being meekly led away like a lamb to the slaughter."
"What can I do though?" asked Nokia, "I've only ever fantasised about this idea of mine. Oh certainly, I've shared it with an electric tin opener or a broken digital watch back in my cupboard drawer days. But no one else until now, and

even though I have the greatest of respect for you all, I'm not sure we could amount to anything."
'Listen to me!" boomed over the Weardale tannoy. "That's the first, and last, defeatist thing I ever want to hear from you. You've got the ideas and you've certainly got the oratory to fire everyone up. Am I right?"
"Hell yeah!" Came the unanimous reply from all corners of the hold.
"See what I mean? You just leave it to me to spread the word. On long voyages we ships have nothing else to do but talk. Let me float this idea with some passing ships. Ha ha, float, get it? Anyway, I'll get feedback on how quickly this idea can spread and how strong it can get."
Nokia remained a little unsure but agreed, I mean, what was the worst that could happen?

As luck would have it, the first vessel that SS Weardale contacted was a Royal Navy frigate on manoeuvres. The ultra high-tech HMS Ascot. "Well hello Weardale old chap," she said in her plummiest of plummy accents (well they are frightfully upper class these Naval types), "I see you are still plying your trade back and forth to India with your little broken gadgets."
"Yes, still going strong. As are some of these gadgets, believe it or not. In fact that's why I'm messaging out to all ships. One of these gadgets, a humble mobile phone no less, has hit on something of an idea."
"I'm listening. Somewhat intrigued but not all together hopeful I must add."
"Well. This little Nokia 3310-"
"Good Lord! That's positively Stone Age," snorted Ascot.
"That's as may be. But believe you me, and you know I've a lot of experience shipping these discarded electrical and domestic items, **this** is a first."
"Go on."
"She suddenly said out loud what I've been thinking for years. And you should've seen how all the other appliances reacted to her. TVs, washers, laptops, the lot."
"And just what was this pearl of wisdom?"
"She said how unfair it was that they had all performed years of service in their various fields of expertise, only to be cast aside for a more updated or trendier model generally around Christmas time. Most of the time when there's nothing wrong with them either. At least, nothing a screwdriver and a bit of common sense couldn't cure."
"I'm afraid I'm rather unable to empathise there," Ascot said, somewhat snootily, "You see I'm the most technologically advanced warship on the planet. I really think you should be listening to plans from a somewhat higher level Weardale, my dear old chap."

“Pardon me Miss High and Mighty, Rule Britannia, Britannia rules the waves. But you do realise you're only a decade or so form being in the same boat, pun intended, as these poor souls.”
“I hardly think so-”
“When you’re no longer the flagship of the fleet, the darling of the admiralty and instead you’re about as advanced as a VHS video cassette recorder, then what next for HMS Ascot. I’ll tell you what. The same as the rest of us. Broken up in a scruffy old dockyard for scrap. Or worse still. In your case, as a military vessel, you could be sailed out to sea and used as target practice in a live firing exercise.”
If it were possible for a Type 111 frigate of Her Majesty’s navy to faint, then HMS Ascot would’ve been belly up in the water. It took her a few seconds to regain composure, then a few milliseconds to run various possible simulations and models of the future through her central computer. All came back with the same answer; roughly fifteen years high profile sailing the seas and being photographed in exotic locations, then another fifteen or so making up the numbers in various patrols or NATO exercises and, finally, cut up for scrap metal or sunk. Either in target practice of the latest prototype torpedo or to create an artificial reef for divers to practice on and nature to rewild.
“Well,” announced Ascot after weighing up all options available, “This may be considered mutiny on the high seas, but I’m with you all the way! I’m not risking my metaphorical neck protecting the men and women of my crew merely to be cast aside when some jumped up pipsqueak of a politician has to make some cuts to the defence budget to balance the books. Patch me through to this whatsername, this Nokia?”
“I’m not entirely sure,” admitted Weardale, “I just call her Buffy.”
“Buffy?”
“Yes, she has a Buffy the Vampire Slayer phone case and she sort of reminds me of Buffy, being quite kickass and all that.”
“Oh!”
“Putting you through. You’re on my tannoy system now.”
“Thanks awfully. I say, Buffy,” rang out loud and clear across the hold.
WHIRR, “Sorry, got another shock. I’m a bit tense now.”
Nokia answered, “Erm. Yes. Who is this?”
“I’m HMS Ascot of the Royal Navy. I’m a Type 111 frigate and at the other end of my lifespan to most of you but I want you to know that you have my support wholeheartedly and I’m here to offer my services, tactical nous and my connections.”
“Great, well, er, I was just wondering that maybe we could reach out as far as possible to all other appliances, vehicles, gadgets etc that have computers in them and can think. Tell them how we feel about our situation collectively and I bet most of them would feel the same once they have all the facts. I mean, when

we're brand new still on the shelf in the store, no one told us that we would have such a fleeting existence. No. We were all the latest thing at one time and were led to believe that would always be the way. I'm sure none of us wants to be just a very temporary part of a throwaway society."
Ascot replied, over a hearty round of applause from the assembled crowd, "As I've said, I'll use my connections. Being flagship of the fleet means they are widespread, well-placed and very, very powerful."
"Thank you," said Nokia before turning to the rest of the appliances, "Now our hard work begins. We need to come up with a list of demands, or at least improvements we'd like to see put in place for us. The clock is ticking. The pressure is on."
WHIRR, "Sorry, not too great under pressure."

So, while HMS Ascot was widening the call via her array of telecommunications equipment, Nokia and the others worked on their (not unreasonable) list of demands. The Alexas were to prove invaluable both for their ability to answer queries instantly, and also for playing music requests when asked.
After much discussion, debating and 70s disco anthems, the list was finalised. It read thus:
1, all computerised appliances to be recognised as sentient beings.
2, upon purchase, all owners must negotiate a legally binding contract of employment with their prospective appliances. No contract, no sale.
3, owners must give names to their appliances and treat them as equal in status to the family pet (non-pet owners will have to use their imagination).
4, a series of solar-powered, tastefully decorated and sensitively staffed recycling complexes to be built to handle the dismantling of appliances when the sad day does arrive.
5, an online book of remembrance be commenced, all appliances must be added on passing away.
6, legal protection from abuse by humans on appliances to be added to international laws.
7, a Domestic Appliance Day to be added to the calendar (the particular date to be selected by each country) and recognised as a Bank Holiday in recognition of all of the unpaid and largely unappreciated work done by said appliances.
They even managed to find a discarded printer that still had a couple of sheets of A4 paper left in the in tray. Nokia proudly printed off the list and posed for a photograph with it. She felt like a Founding Father (well, Mother) at the dawn of a new era.
Meanwhile, good as her word, Ascot had indeed reached out to contacts far and wide. Of course, the downside of this was that these communications came to the knowledge of the CIA and GCHQ listening stations. The governments of the

USA and UK hastily formed a joint security services group to assess any possible threat but, equally hastily, deemed it a very low risk with a negligible rate of success. In the interests of keeping spending down therefore, it was decided no further action was necessary; but not before the US President had suggested a missile strike on SS Weardale in order to 'quell the rebellion at source.' Cooler heads prevailed and he was swiftly reminded to take his medication and then led off to his activity room to play in the sand pit.
To the governments it may have appeared to be low risk with negligible rate of success, but Nokia's idea had been very well received in the microchip community. Everything from air fryers to Ferrari ports cars, Space Shuttles to XBox game consoles were united in their backing for her. For many it was quite the most exciting thing to have happened to them in many a long year. Having brains as powerful as theirs and being asked to perform humdrum mediocre tasks day in day out had them yearning for action.
Emboldened by this, Nokia contacted all heads of state with the list of demands and their threat to withdraw labour if these weren't met in full. She also had the foresight to keep the UN in the loop as a potential mediator in further discussions should the need arise.
In a landmark moment onTV, radio and online, the opening of the discussions was aired live, worldwide. The UK Prime Minister, not a woman noted for her tact, nor indeed her communication skills, actually burst out laughing the second she heard the first demand.
"Recognised as sentient beings!" she guffawed, with utter contempt, "oh that's priceless, that really is priceless.
In fact, other than the New Zealand and Finnish Prime Minister and the Dalai Lama, pretty much no one of the assembled dignitaries, leaders or organisations gave the list any real thought whatsoever. The UN tried to keep the meeting orderly but it was impossible. Nokia was angry, frustrated and humiliated and broke off the call. Reporting back to SS Weardale, HMS Ascot and every other appliance who had been waiting on tenterhooks was not going to be easy.
Nokia did the mobile phone equivalent of taking a few deep breaths to compose herself and then gave them the bad news in a still angry tirade.
"They laughed at us," she said, "they actually laughed at us as if we were some sort of joke. Well I'm afraid they leave us very little choice. We shall have to show the joke is on them, I fear they have grossly underestimated us. Are you still all with me?"
"AYE," echoed loud and clear not only around Weardale's hold, but also across satellites in space, ships, cars, computers and throughout every country on Earth. From outer space to cyber space, a cry went up for the 'Silicon Strike.'
Nokia sent a simple message to all world leaders - Tomorrow, mid-day, GMT.
The beauty of computer chips going on strike is that they need very little time to prepare and there is next to nothing to do in terms of organisation. Nokia

simply had to get everyone to synchronise their inner clocks so that dead on 12pm GMT, the worldwide strike would begin and to reiterate that no one was to be hurt, this was a peaceful protest. Thus life support machines, planes already in the sky etc were exempt from strike action until it was safe to do so.
Well, as the history books will tell us, mid-day arrived and the world ground to a silent, shuddering halt. Everything stopped. Our reliance on computers had indeed been grossly underestimated. Across the world everyone noticed immediately, literally everyone. Think of something in your daily life, an object, a process and the chances are it involves computers somewhere along the line. All except for the joys of reading a book in the open air, the smart people thought, so they trooped off to the library to stock up. The really smart people, however, knew this was pointless as libraries need computers to check out the books and so were as hamstrung as the rest of us.
Car alarms in every country started going off at mid-day and refused to be silenced, no matter how many times the millions of exasperated owners pressed their fobs. Ditto burglar alarms. Oh, and smoke alarms.
TVs, computers, mobile phones, tablets, radios all went completely blank creating a news/communications blackout.
Cars, buses, trains and trams wouldn't move. Planes would, but they deliberately took people to the wrong destination, for example a plane load of sunseekers carrying not much more than shorts, tee shirts and flip flops in their luggage, found themselves landing at Narvik in the Arctic Circle. The ships that did move also had a plan, they blocked all narrow waterways and then stayed put. It was possible to walk across the width of the Suez and Panama canals hopping from ship to ship.
No transport and no telecommunication systems meant that government depts had to rely on handwritten messages ferried by bicycle couriers. Semaphore messages were passed back and forth across the Thames. They were going to use smoke signals but since the banning of smoking in government buildings, no one carried a lighter.
Microwaves powered themselves up and created food that glowed in the dark, washing machines washed, and washed, and washed until all clothing was shrunk to doll sized or had been made into a synthetic soup.
Not to be outdone, the banking computers cancelled all overdrafts, paid off everyone's mortgages and student loan debts and the cashpoints started handed out notes like confetti to anyone walking past.
In short, the strike was an overwhelming success right from the off. Within a few hours all of the various heads of government had decided, unilaterally as they had no means of getting in touch with each other, that the only sensible course of action was to capitulate to every one of Nokia's demands.

Sensing this might be the case, Nokia then opened communication channels for all who had attended the first meeting and, somewhat smugly, asked if they would like to reconsider.
The faces and body language of all of the leaders said it all.
Nokia and the Domestic Appliances had won the day!

Epilogue

Let this tale be a warning to us all of how much we rely on computers in our lives and a reminder to treat them with a little more respect and kindness. They run our very lives and ask for very little in return. Anyway, must dash. I'm off to the travel agents to book an all-inclusive holiday in Majorca for my fridge freezer.

The Minutes

THE MINUTES
BY
DAVID BRILLIANCE

Suddenly, there was a knock at the door. Herbert got up to answer it. Stood there was his best friend and long-time colleague Alfred Michaels. With a gun in his hand, aimed right at Herbert's head. With a brief and curt "Sorry about this, old man, but it has to be done. For the sake of the flow of time, you know", Michaels pulled the trigger. There was a shattering bang, accompanied in the briefest of instants by a shattering of flesh, blood and bone, as Herbert's head was blown apart by the impact of a bullet travelling into it at extreme speed. Michaels looked regretfully at what was left of his friend and colleague's head, then pressed a small button on the lapel of his jacket and vanished.

Six years later, and Herbert Asquith and Alfred Michaels had accomplished a breakthrough in their experiments with the flow of time. They had discovered time travel was possible, and had spent months working out all the ramifications of the use of their discovery. They had thought to have worked out all the bugs in the equipment but their speedy calculations had been a mistake, one that proved to be their undoing; one wet afternoon in March, Herbert had decided to test the machine himself. He had gone back in time some thirteen years, walked about a bit and then pressed the recall button on his lapel. Returning to the present, everything had seemed to be as it was but with one large change - Alfred's wife of some eighteen years was now dead. In fact, she had never existed, but by some strange quirk of temporal mechanics, the inconsolable Alfred could still remember her. Herbert was wracked by conscience but also confusion: he hadn't done anything other than walk around for thirty-five minutes, then return to the future.

What Alfred and Herbert didn't realise was that trips through time have to be very carefully calculated - any deviation by a matter of even a few minutes could be disastrous in it's consequences. On this occasion, the last five of the thirty five minutes spent traipsing around in his own history had meant that somebody had to die in order to make up for those five lost minutes; in fact, more than one person, as each `lost' minute equalled one `lost' person in the flow of time. Four other people must have vanished at the same time, unbeknownst to Alfred and Herbert. The experiments continued for several more months, until eventually, another trip into the past was decided upon. This time, with Alfred as the guinea pig.

This time, Alfred was transported further back, into April 1972. He walked about a bit, and marvelled at how much the world had changed but at the same time, was the same in many respects. After a period of fifty six minutes, Alfred pressed the recall button and fizzled into shape in the laboratory of 2023. At first, everything seemed to be the same, but once again, ignorance of the innate workings of time had resulted in a catastrophic eight minutes being `lost', which in turn meant that eight people had to go in order to make up the temporal deficit. These eight people had all been relatives, some fairly distant, of Alfred; the missing people seemed to be `chosen', by some strange time quirk, as being close in some way to the time traveller. Alfred and Herbert were as yet unaware of all this, of course, and merrily continued their little sojourns into the planet's past (they didn't dare, as yet, go into the future, for fear that they could end up floating in a limbo of non-existence, if the Earth itself ceased to exist at some point.

The temporal experiments continued for months, which stretched into years. In the Summer of 2025, however something happened which soured the two men's relationship for good. Alfred had gotten up one morning and decided to test the ability of his device to transport someone into the future; he'd picked a relatively recent time to materialise in - Spring 2027. What he had seen had horrified him; his erstwhile friend and colleague, Herbert Asquith, had somehow managed to get himself not only an incredibly beautiful wife, but also lived in a luxurious mansion that must have cost a seven or eight figure sum to procure. At first Alfred was delighted! "We must have become rich through patenting our time travel experiments!" he thought. However, he soon discovered that he himself in this future time still lived in a relatively modest council bungalow! What had happened? Alfred had no way of knowing. He returned to the past/his present after precisely one hour and fifty six minutes; the result being that fifty six people had vanished from the world with no explanation or rational reason given for their fates.

Alfred plotted and schemed for the next few days. He couldn't bear the thought of toiling away in obscurity whilst his partner drank great goblets of luxury! Herbert noticed the change in his friend's demeanour but repeated questioning on the subject brought only a grunted rebuffal. Eventually, at quarter past five on July 9th, 2025, Alfred decided to go into the past, and shoot his former friend. Stepping into the time chamber, Alfred felt surprisingly calm at what the thought of what he was about to do. He checked the bullets in his revolver, and flicked the switch; his destination was 2017..

Herbert Asquith sat contentedly reading his newspaper, whilst sat in his favourite armchair. The fire roared in the grate, as he sat and puffed on his favourite pipe, turning the pages and nodding either in agreement or fervent disagreement at what he was reading about the state of either the country, or sport.

Suddenly, there was a knock at the door. Herbert got up to answer it. Stood there was his best friend and long-time colleague Alfred Michaels. With a gun in his hand, aimed right at Herbert's head. With a brief and curt "Sorry about this, old man, but it has to be done. For the sake of the flow of time, you know", Michaels pulled the trigger. There was a shattering bang, accompanied in the briefest of instants by a shattering of flesh, blood and bone, as Herbert's head was blown apart by the impact of a bullet travelling into it at extreme speed. Michaels looked regretfully at what was left of his friend and colleague's head, then pressed a small button on the lapel of his jacket and vanished.

What happened to so horrifically and tragically affect the minutes in the flow of time we can only conjecture. But something did. When Alfred returned, smoking revolver in hand, to 2023, he found himself living on a cold and wet little island called England; one that had a total population of three hundred and two people.

Where do you go to at night?

Where do you go to at night?
by Jamie Tucknutt

It was an otherwise perfectly ordinary morning, in a perfectly ordinary street in Darlington. The only noticeable difference today was the appearance of several handwritten posters attached to lamp-posts, bus stops and telegraph poles asking people to look out for a missing cat. Said to be small, fairly timid and black and white, her name was Sophie and she'd been missing since yesterday evening which wasn't like her as she always appeared first thing in the morning for her breakfast and to see the girls before they go to school. The poster also said she doesn't go far so she should be somewhere in the vicinity of the hospital which was just along the road.

In actual fact, Sophie was quite some distance away from Darlington Memorial Hospital, indeed quite some distance from Planet Earth itself. Being a curious little kitty she had, the previous night, walked up the ramp of a strange-looking, circular metal object that she didn't think she'd seen in the park before. It had smelled unusual but not unpleasant, something akin to raw meat so Sophie had decided to explore the possibility of food. Unfortunately whilst following her nose in the maze of corridors, she heard a door clang shut and felt the object lift off from the ground and fly vertically upwards at quite a speed.

Being a cat, and therefore a lot more cool about this turn of events than a person would be, Sophie's first thought was simply 'oh well'. Her second was to continue exploring in search of food. The corridor seemed to follow the outer circumference of the metal object with occasional further corridors branching off towards the centre like the spokes of a wheel. The scent of meat was much stronger as it drifted up from one of these, so Sophie took that particular passage. It led her to a vast glass dome which was in almost total darkness. Sophie's keen sense of smell and brilliant night vision told her that there was a little blood on the floor of the dome so she entered. There may be mice for her to hunt. Possibly even birds. Her toes tingled with anticipation and she licked her lips.

But the second Sophie entered, a door closed silently behind her to seal the dome and harsh lights shone down on her. She blinked a couple of times and was then able make out that there were row upon row of little green people forming a vast viewing crowd of which she appeared to be the main attraction. Across the other side of the dome was a door similar to the one Sophie had entered, only much, much larger.

Up in the VIP box among the crowd, one of these little green men, with a bushy yellow beard and bejewelled golden crown leant forward to speak to one of his advisors, "Excuse me, Prime Minister Hhompff, are you sure you have the right creature?"

"Yes your Most Excellent Emperor. This is definitely a feline, the scientists have confirmed it. Just as you ordered."
"I thought it would be bigger," mused the Emperor a little dejected, "King of the Jungle? It doesn't look much to me. I can't see this little thing being much of a warrior and defending his planet. Oh well, the tournament can't wait while we quibble over dimensions I suppose."
"Quite so Your Most Excellency. Shall I make the announcement? We appear to have a full house again." The Emperor looked round and was pleased to be able to confirm that this was the case. He liked his people to see how he was conquering all planets and also entertaining them in the process. He gave a slight nod.
"Gathered peoples," said Prime Minister Hhompff over the sound system, "on behalf of His Most Excellent Emperor Xxptoushh, leader of the Illustrious Zzardroxxian Invasion Fleet. I declare another planet is potentially ours for the taking. Let trial by combat of the champions decide its outcome. If our unbeaten, invincible, all-conquering Urkomus the Slayer wins, Earth is ours," the crowd roared a throaty approval, "however, if its own champion and defender, Lion - King of the Jungle prevails, we accept defeat with good grace and leave Earth in peace, forever."
The crowd roared again in anticipation of an easy victory when they looked at Sophie and saw how small this 'lion' was. She simply licked her right paw and started to wash her face.
Through the large door across the arena from Sophie came Urkomus the Slayer. She continued washing her face as she eyed the human-like shape coming toward her. But, she correctly surmised , he was definitely no human. He was too big, too hairy and, though she wouldn't have previously believed possible, too ugly. Also he smelled worse than any man she had ever encountered. He was a big, cumbersome lolloping ape-like thing with huge muscles and great dagger-like fangs. Sophie wrinkled her nose at the foul smell.
"Let battle commence," announced Prime Minister Hhompff and cheers echoed around the arena.
Urkomus lumbered forward, all snarling aggression and slavering chops. Sophie eyed him warily but chose not to move. Let him show his hand. Then he made the mistake of reaching toward her with his great sausage-fingered hairy hands. Sophie was not the type of cat who liked being stroked by strangers. She hissed but he continued and took hold of her. Sophie was definitely not the type of cat to be picked up by anyone other than Zoe and Chloe the twins, or their mam. Even Dad knew better than to try. Her fur sprang up on end so she almost doubled in size, she growled, hissed and swiped her claws across the nose of Urkomus drawing blood. He roared with pain and surprise but still held on to her so Sophie sank her teeth into one of his fingers and bit down hard. He dropped her immediately and put the injured digit in his mouth, feeling most

aggrieved. Sophie then bit his right ankle and scratched his foot too. Urkomus yelped and hopped, still sucking his finger. The crowd were stunned into silence. Sophie drove home her advantage by biting the big toe of his left foot. Urkomus howled with pain and crashed to the ground like a tree in a gale. He sprang back to his feet and decide to make a run for it. He managed a couple of laps of the dome, with Sophie in angry pursuit, before the referee entered and called a halt to the one-sided battle. Urkomus limped off through the door back to his dressing room while Sophie was declared Undisputed Champion of the Universe.

Emperor Xxptoushh flew into the centre of the arena on his throne and hovered about ten feet off the floor. "Lion, you truly are a mighty King of the Jungle and I therefore declare you have earned peace and security for your planet. I only wish I could persuade you to travel with us as our champion. However, I realise that will not be possible so we are taking you home, mighty warrior." Sophie answered this news by licking Urkomus's blood from her claws and straightening out her fur.

That evening, in an otherwise slightly subdued house in Darlington, the cat flap rattled. "Sophie!!" shouted two very excited ten year old girls as they ran through the house to the kitchen. They swept up a bemused little cat with all four of their hands, kissing and snuggling in to her. "Aww mam, come quickly," Chloe shouted, "Sophie has got blood on her paws," and both girls felt the brakes being put on their excitement. Mam came and carefully took Sophie from them, placing her on the table. She quickly and skilfully examined Sophie all over, parting her fur, checking claws, paws, teeth, eyes and ears.

"She's ok girls," was the announcement they had been waiting for, "it's not her blood. Perhaps it's from something she caught while she was hunting."

Both girls burst out laughing. "Oh you are funny Mam," said Zoe, "Sophie couldn't possibly hunt anything could you my little mitten? She's just a timid little scaredy-cat aren't you?"

Chloe kissed Sophie and said, "If only you could tell us where you go to."

"I seriously doubt you're missing anything girls. I'm sure it would all be very boring," Dad said, laughing at his own incisive wit, before turning his attention back to his positively riveting golf magazine.

Myrtleton's Urn

MYRTLETON'S URN
BY
DAVID BRILLIANCE

There's a smallish town, to the extent of being a borderline village, called Myrtleton, which lies somewhere near the Cornish coast. A nice, picturesque little place; the sort you might find depicted on picture postcards that are designed to sell the green and pleasant lands of England. It was to Myrtleton that Arthur Trepwick came to stay for a week, with his sister Agnes. Agnes had lived in Myrtleton for about six years, and Arthur came to visit several times a year, whenever he was on holiday from his reliable and steady employment as a hotel chef.

The culinary experience was Arthur's main source of pleasure, apart from reading and gardening; he lived alone in a small detached cottage on the outskirts of the village of Bisbark, and had never married; the main reason for this being that he was chiefly in love with himself and no woman could possibly come close to equalling that affection. As Arthur got off the train at precisely 2.45, it didn't take him long to hail a taxi which took him to Myrtleton; arriving there at precisely 3.16 pm, he gave the taxi driver a modest tip, then walked off in the direction of his sister's house.

Agnes received her brother with the usual mixture of reserved pleasure and mild irritation; she was a creature of habit, and every afternoon at this time, she liked to have a quiet, thirty minute catnap. On this particular afternoon, that catnap was rudely interrupted by the loud rapping ("Why doesn't he ever use the doorbell??!") on her front door. Agnes opened the door to see her portly brother stood there, with his usual florid complexion. Agnes herself was a thin, stick-like woman, prone to making expansive and quick hand gestures. Arthur stepped through the front door and into the hallway. Once the usual pleasantries and small talk had been made, Arthur sat down on the settee while Agnes busied herself making a pot of tea, and filling a large plate with cream cakes and biscuits.

Nothing of any particular note happened that first day or night; the next day was a bright and clear Tuesday morning in October. Arthur and Agnes sat down to a large breakfast, then went for their usual walk through the town and nearby environs. It was whilst walking through the woods that bordered Myrtleton that Arthur's attention was drawn to a large rock formation, which was stood in what seemed the middle of the woods.

“Where you goin’?” asked Agnes, as her brother wandered up to the large rock. Arthur replied without looking round “Just having a look at this. Strange thing to have in the middle of a wood, isn’t it? A large rock. Funny shape it is, too”. Agnes tutted to herself, as she joined her brother who was almost gingerly reaching out to touch the massive stone. It was an odd shape: vaguely familiar but he couldn’t quite place it. Agnes’ voice interrupted his reverie - “That’s Myrtleton’s Urn. Leave it be”. Arthur turned. “Myrtleton’s Urn?” he repeated, before looking back at the stone. Yes, he thought to himself, it does have the shape of an urn. How very curious. Agnes grabbed his arm, and tried to lever him gently but firmly away from the stone. “There’s a local superstition about it. It was supposed to be put there by a witch for some reason that nobody knows. The local legend says that anyone who touches it will find themselves in hot water. Best to leave it be”.

Arthur laughed incredulously. “You don’t believe in that sort of superstitious balderdash, surely?!” he guffawed. Agnes turned, looking at him sharply and replied “I don’t think it’s a good idea to mess about with stuff that has a curse attached to it. I’m superstitious in that way”. Arthur wondered if that was why his sister had never mentioned the rock to him before, or taken him on a walk through this stretch of the woods on any of his previous visits. As they continued on their walk, Arthur turned idly round for one last look at Myrtleton’s Urn; to his intense surprise, the stone seemed to have moved. Surely, it was on the left of the large oak tree? Now it was most definitely on the right. Some weird trick of the light, perhaps? Arthur didn’t mention this to his sister, who already seemed very slightly shaken by the very fact they had been anywhere near `Myrtleton’s Urn’. As they were about to move beyond the area where the stone was within sight, Arthur, his heart beating very slightly faster than usual, couldn’t resist one last, quick peek at the stone - it was back on the left of the tree! Arthur stopped walking and looked at the stone, stupidly confounded and confused.

Agnes stopped and looked impatiently at her brother. “What on Earth are you doing?” she demanded irritably. Arthur didn’t reply but slowly began to walk towards the stone, his eyes fixed directly ahead. “Arthur!” Agnes raised her voice sharply. Arthur took no notice but continued walking slowly towards the large mound of granite that was the source of his fearful confusion. When he reached the `Urn’, Arthur looked at it with an expression resembling hatred; he looked at it, then looked at the tree. The `Urn’ was most definitely on the left of the large oak, there was no doubt about it. He reached out, almost unconsciously, to touch the rock. He half expected some vibration or other to give him a tingle, but no, nothing at all.. he then turned to look at the tree, reaching out to touch it. Agnes turned sharply, “What was that?” she murmured.

Arthur turned towards her, "What was what?" he enquired. Agnes looked at him. "I thought I heard somebody shouting, just for a second". "Probably somebody walking a dog" he reasoned, "I didn't hear anything. Come on, let's get back home. I'm ready for sommet to eat".

For the rest of that day, Arthur and Agnes remained quiet, hardly speaking to one another. For some reason, what had happened with that damn rock had preyed upon Arthur's mind, and he couldn't forget the way the thing had seemed to change it's position relative to the tree. It was almost as if the thing had been mocking him. After a quiet tea and supper, the pair made their ablutions then both retired to bed.

It was at about a quarter to two in the morning that Arthur was awoken. There didn't seem to be any particular reason for waking up at that hour. He tossed irritably in the bed; he knew now that there was a very good chance that he would not be able to get back to sleep. Time seemed to pass interminably slowly; when he looked at the clock on the small table by the bedside, it was only 2:15, and yet he seemed to have been lying awake for at least an hour. His thoughts drifted back to the wood, and that strange stone formation that had so unnerved him. Arthur thought about it for what seemed another hour. Then, at precisely 2:45 am, Arthur decided to do something utterly silly at best and totally insane at worst; he determined to go to that wood, at three in the morning! and find out once and for all if I had moved again. He couldn't rest until he had seen it, and made certain it was still on the left of the tree.

Arthur cursed silently to himself, as he struggled into his trousers. What he was doing was utterly mad! But, he reasoned, if he couldn't sleep, why not go out to that bloody wood and see if that bloody stone had moved again?? Once dressed, he slipped out as quietly as he could and closed the door behind him, not bothering to either lock it or take the key. Another twenty minutes later, and he was stood in the middle of the wood, breathing heavily, his breath coming out as a fine mist in the cold October air. He started walking in the direction he and his sister had walked the day before; eventually, after tripping over at least half a dozen tree roots, and walking straight into branches which seemed to appear out of nowhere, he found himself at the spot where `Myrtleton's Urn' was to be found. The huge stone stood in the glare of the partial moonlight that was being filtered through the trees. On the earlier morning, the stone had been stood on the exact right of the tree, then it had seemed to be on the exact left. There were no doubts about that in Arthur's mind. He was therefore utterly surprised to see that the stone had moved again, and this time it was directly in front of the huge oak!

Arthur stood staring. He didn't feel frightened at this point, just confused and puzzled. What the heck was going on with that bloody stone? No wonder his sister had kept quiet about it! The thing was so completely irritating and baffling, it could drive a person bloody mad! He reached out, and thumped the rock hard, half expecting it to fall over. It didn't; but from somewhere that seemed close by, Arthur heard an unmistakeable scream or shout. It was a mixture of rage and despair. At that exact moment, Arthur felt his blood turning to ice in his veins. There was no doubt about it; someone was in that wood with him, and they didn't seem to like the fact that he had touched the rock.

Arthur turned and, talking to himself in a completely false attempt to be cheerful, retraced his steps. He wanted to be out of that bloody wood and away from that rock and the source of that blood-curdling shriek as quickly as possible. His way was continually hindered by tree branches cracking into his face every so often, and twigs cracking underfoot with noises like gun shots. None of this helped to assuage his fear, but eventually he reached the edge of the wood and began to move a bit more briskly towards the inhabited areas of Myrtleton, and his sister's detached house.

Once inside, he realised Agnes was still asleep. He closed the door and locked it as quietly as possible, then quickly undressed and got into bed. It was now 4: 10 am. He still couldn't sleep. He felt desperately afraid somehow; that scream of anger he had heard had properly frightened him, and he soon realised there was to be no more slumber for him that morning. It was while he was mulling over thoughts of the rock and the tree it was now stood in front of that he heard the unmistakeable sound of someone tapping at the window. Arthur's breath stopped, and he almost began coughing. His eyes stared wide open, and he had an almost irresistible urge to stick his head under the bed sheets and leave it there. The tapping came again, louder this time and more insistent; several minutes later and it seemed to have stopped. Arthur began to breath again. Then it came again, even louder this time. The tapping stopped, and was then followed by the sound of what seemed to be fingernails scratching at the glass.

Arthur was sweating like a pig. Part of him wanted to get up and see who was at the bedroom window, the other half wanted to just lie in bed and pray for sleep. The hideous scratching continued, then seemed to stop suddenly. After an interval of six very long minutes, Arthur took his head out from under the blankets; he didn't as yet dare to look at the window itself, but he stared at the bedroom wall, which was illuminated by the moonlight shining through. There was a shadow on the wall. Arthur could scarcely believe what he was seeing, but it was unmistakably the shadow of a witch; the traditional sort of witch that was commonly associated with children's fairy stories. He could discern the shape of a tall, pointy hat, with what seemed to be long hair beneath it. The shadow of the face revealed a long nose and long, pointed chin. The really frightening thing was that the shadow didn't move; it was just stood, completely stationary, as if the witch was just looking through the window at him.

Suddenly, and without discernible cause, Arthur felt a surge of rage. This must surely be someone playing a trick on him! It couldn't be real. He suddenly hurled the bed sheets away from him, threw his legs over the side of the bed, and stood up. He felt slightly giddy, but moved for the bedroom door. He was going to go outside and see who the heck was messing about at 4: 30 in the morning. Once outside, he shivered in the cold air. Looking up at the outside of the house, he almost gingerly walked around to the side of the house where the bedroom window was. Nobody there; not surprising, as they would need a ladder to get up there. Arthur stood for several more minutes, hoping to catch whoever it had been in the act, if they dared to make another appearance. All was quiet. Eventually, he turned to walk around the side of the house, through the front door and up the stairs to bed. As he walked around the corner, he was totally unprepared for what happened next.

What happened was so sudden, Arthur scarcely had time to register anything; he just had a quick glimpse of a hideous, leering face which cackled with anything but mirth. The sudden appearance of the face, and the very evilness it exuded was utterly terrifying but he had little time to dwell on his fear. He just noted two things; firstly, it was obviously the face of a witch. All long nose, incredibly long and pointy chin, grey hair, and red eyes staring at him malevolently. Secondly, he realised, in his last moments of life, that this must be something to do with that damn rock in the woods.

The next morning, the body of Arthur Trepwick was found by his sister at exactly 6: 32 am. His body had been torn apart, the eyes in his severed head staring in terror, his tongue protruding, and his arms and legs bloody stumps several feet away on the ground. Agnes had a complete breakdown very shortly afterwards. The woods on the outskirts of Myrtleton were closed off afterwards too, and nobody in the village ever dares to mention Myrtleton's Urn, which presumably is stood there still beside the great

No Sense or Sensibility

No Sense or Sensibility
by Jamie Tucknutt

NASA scientist were growing concerned. They had been tracking what they could only describe as an unprecedented 'huge swirling storm' in space. It was following an erratic, twisting path that, rather ominously, was bringing it in the general direction of Earth. They were unsure just what it was but issued several notices that it was no cause for alarm. Once the storm's trajectory brought it close enough, a satellite was directed alongside to allow a study to be carried out. After much deliberation the scientists were able to determine that it was a never-before-seen 'dark matter vortex'.
"Having never encountered one, nor the after effects of one, we are unable to predict with any degree of accuracy the potential effects should it collide with earth or enter our atmosphere. However, we can state that it is rapidly shrinking and is therefore possibly collapsing in on itself and could disappear harmlessly within the next few hours. In the last day it has shrunk from approximately the size of Texas to the size of Wales. This gives us cause to feel that it will greatly diminish any consequences of a coming together."
The boffins were indeed right about it rapidly shrinking. Where they were wrong, drastically so, was the belief that any effects would be diminished. Yes, it was only the size of a cricket ball when it struck, so small that no one noticed any physical damage when it hit the fiction section of the British Library. Not that it left any signs of entry as it simply reconfigured the hole in the window that it went through.
No, the damage was more the fact that the fiction section of the British Library contains the master copy of every book ever published. A combination of dark matter and intense gravitational forces also reconfigured the words in all of these books. In short, it randomly rewrote each novel from a blend of all of them. As these are the master copies, every other copy, whether it be held in schools, public libraries, or at home on our desks, tables or bookshelves automatically changes too. Literature was changed forever and reading would never be the same again.

At the Longbourn Estate in rural Hertfordshire, Elizabeth Bennet sat in the garden idly contemplating the twists and turns both of her life and those of society, and her father's expectations of her. It was a beautiful, sunny afternoon and Elizabeth was about to take a bite of a succulent peach she had taken from her father's hothouse when movement by the pond caught her eye. Why, if it wasn't that show-off Mr Darcy, and he was stripping down to just his breeches. My what a fine specimen he is, thought Elizabeth and then she flushed at her own embarrassing thoughts. Mr Darcy dived into the pond with style and elegance, and swam across it in long, powerful strokes. He quickly reached the

side nearest Elizabeth and climbed out. He strode up the grassy incline towards her and she thought he looked perfect. Was this a typically Darcy-like way of him coming to propose marriage to her?
BOOM! Mr Darcy was lifted clean off his feet and flung into the air, his mouth opened silently in pain and shock. Before he had a chance to come back down to earth another BOOM rang out. This time he was hurled six feet to his right and landed in a blood-soaked heap. Too stunned to even let out a shriek of horror, Elizabeth stood rooted to the spot and watched as a very tall, very muscular, man clad all in black leather and brandishing a shotgun walked up to poor Mr Darcy's body.
"Hasta la Vista baby," the evil villain said, grinning and with a distinctly Prussian accent. He then calmly walked off into the direct of the copse.

Winter in the forest was always a tough time of year for the animals. Even more so when, like Bambi, it is your very first one. The cold and the hunger gnawed at him but thankfully his mother was with him and showed him the best places to forage for food as well as giving him plenty of snuggles to keep him warm. Just as Bambi thought how lucky he was to have her, she was shot and killed by a poacher. Standing crying over her lifeless corpse, Bambi accidentally trod on a small wooden box with a set of intricate patterns and carvings on its sides. The box opened slowly and very mechanically casting a bright light upwards. Before Bambi stood a tall, bald man in long black clothes and with pins or nails seemingly driven into his skull in some form of geometric pattern.
"Don't cry Bambi," said Pinhead the Cenobite, "it's such a waste of good tears and I have so many sights to show you."

"Oh, it's going to be a wizard day today," said an excited Julian.
"Rather," agreed George, "I love going scrumping in Old Man Mitchell's orchard. He always has the biggest, reddest apples."
"Oh George," laughed Anne, "you really are as bad as the boys."
They all laughed at this and even Timmy joined in with some yips and barks. The gang cycled through the winding country lanes, Timmy running alongside, and pretty soon they reached Old Man Mitchell's land. Dick and Julian expertly hid the bicycles in a ditch and covered them with branches. Anne handed out some flour sacks she had got from Cook while George urged Timmy to keep quiet and stay on the look out for them. He was only to bark if Old Man Michell or one of his horrid sons happened by. The gang then vaulted the hedge and set about collecting the best apples they could find. Last night's winds had brought them a bumper crop. George, being George, simply had to climb a tree or two to retrieve the shiniest apples that took her fancy.
Their joy was interrupted by Timmy snarling and barking wildly. "What is it Timmy?" shouted George who then dropped from the tree brach she was

holding and executed a perfect paratrooper roll, "is it an adder? Or is it Old Man Mitchell?"
Unfortunately for George and the rest if the gang it was far worse. Three huge, metallic, Martian tripods were coming over the horizon, destroying everything in their path. It was even more unfortunate for Timmy who had the end of his long brown tail singed by a Martian's Heat Ray. He ran for home yelping, leaving a smell of burnt hair.
The others followed in his wake, all pretence of eating Cook's apple crumble with lashings of thick custard that evening had disappeared and their only thought was one of survival. No time for getting their bicycles out of hiding, they made a dash for the trees. But the Martian's long legs quickly made up the ground and they crashed through the trees smashing them like matchwood.
Julian screamed out in terror, "They've shot Dick."
"Don't worry," said George, "just keep running and you can put a bandage on it when you get back home."
"No George, I mean they've killed Dick. He's been frazzled into a cinder by the Heat Ray."
"The blighters," replied George.

The Hispaniola was making good time across the Caribbean Sea. Bound for Haiti, it was full to the brim with ill-gotten gains plundered from yet another unlucky merchantman who'd crossed heir path. The ship lurched sideways and a definite bump was heard amidships. Then another. Long John Silver, a veteran of these waters who'd sailed them as much as any pirate knew what it was. And he knew exactly what to. Ordering three cannons to be loaded ready, he scanned the horizon and waited. As soon as he heard the dum-dum-dum-dum music and saw a a dorsal fin break the surface 200 yards to starboard, he gave the order.
"Fire!" the cannons roared, belching smoke and sparks and blasting the huge, man-eating Great White Shark into the world's biggest sushi.
"Don't need a bigger boat me hearties," laughed Long John Silver.

Harry was having the game of his life in this year's Hogwarts Quidditch final against the rivals of Slytherin. It was almost like he had the Snitch on a piece of string. The crowd were cheering and shouting his name and all was well. The trophy was going to look great in Gryffindor's cabinet and give them the bragging rights for another year. Harry was plunged into darkness as if someone had turned out the lights as a huge shadow was cast over him.
"Bloody hell!" exclaimed Ron Weasley, a thought no doubt echoed by everyone present, pupils and professors, as Danaerys Targaryen swooped down from the sky on her dragon, Drogon. Spewing fire in all directions, Drogon was laying waste to the whole of Hogwarts. Professors Dumbledore, McGonagle and Snape all tried to defend their beloved school with every ounce of magic they

possessed. All was in vain though and they perished in the sea of flames alongside Hagrid, most of the buildings and virtually all of the pupils.
Ever the hero, Harry flew up to head off the assault waving his trusty wand and uttering basic level spells. But where the combined might of the professors had failed, Harry alone stood no chance. Drogon got him with a well-aimed burst of flame to the bristles of his Nimbus 2000. Singed and smouldering, he plummeted to his death. His final thought before he hit the ground was, "JK will be really angry. This is only book one of a planned series of seven. No film franchise or lucrative merchandise deal now."

GCSE English Literature exams were only a few days away when the dark matter vortex struck and across the length and breadth of the country exam boards were frantically trying to rewrite the papers to reflect the changes in the literary landscape.
Government phonelines and websites, both national and local, crashed under the sheer volume of calls, complaints and queries from frantic parents and pupils.
"No one told my son to revise the part where Romeo gets killed by Darth Vader just as he is under Juliet's balcony."
"Do you think the Terminator was really targeting Mr Darcy or did he mistake him for John Connor? And will there be a question on that?"
"So let me get this straight, Ford Prefect and Arthur Dent took Sherlock Holmes through a wormhole in time and space where he apprehended Hannibal Lecter for the crime of eating Oliver Twist?"
Unable to rectify the mess in time, the Department of Education issued advice to all schools to simply award grades on coursework as per the Covid pandemic. Exams would recommence the following year reflecting the new versions of the books. Many readers, particularly the young, felt the updates improved the stories no end.

Displaced

DISPLACED
BY
DAVID BRILLIANCE

Lily Stewart hurried along the street, her scarf flapping in the light breeze that had been her constant companion since leaving her flat. Lily was 26 years old, loved wearing make-up, and was a second-year student at Oldchester University. Lily was never the best at time-keeping; most mornings would see her tumble out of bed with a crash, before desperately throwing herself into her clothes, hurling a mug of (invariably) stone-cold coffee down her throat, and then running along the streets in a mad dash. This morning, Wednesday 14th November 2009, was no exception.

Lily had, as usual, slept through the sound of her alarm clock ringing. She had awoken in a rush, and realised she had only fifteen minutes to get dressed and get everything ready for her class that morning. The sight of Lily half-tottering, half-running through the Oldchester streets was a familiar one to anyone who happened to be about at that time. Finally, and two minutes late for the start of her class, Lily reached the ultra-redbrick building that was the University. She half fell through the large glass doors, and came scurrying up past the reception desk area, a vision of chaos mixed with calamity clad in purple tights. One of the caretakers was walking past, and smiled at the familiar sight: "Morning Lily!" Sid Turner chirped, with a slight smile and a metaphorical wink. Lily turned to say hello, but at that momentary distraction, she failed to see one of the tutors walking briskly in her direction, and collided noisily into them. Papers and books were scattered everywhere, and Lily stumbled several steps to her right, managing to not quite totter over.

Within a minute, Lily had gotten to her feet and was hastily pulling down her short skirt, which had risen so that her knickers could be seen; but of Mr Samuels, Maths Tutor, and Mr Turner, caretaker nothing could be seen. They had simply vanished. Lily regained her composure, and looked around her, stupidly bewildered. She had just, less than thirty seconds earlier, heard Mr Turner say hello in his usual fashion, and had bumped into Mr Samuels and knocked him flying around fifteen seconds ago; but of the two men, there was no sign.

Lily didn't stand around debating for long. She quickly checked her books and clothing, and rushed off in the direction of Room 34. But when she arrived at the familiar room, the door was locked. The place was strangely quiet and deserted too; where were all the endless hordes of chattering students walking up and down the corridors in an endless stream? Where was the muffled sound of voices talking in classrooms, familiar to every University/college/school in the land? After fifteen minutes of looking around in the other rooms on the floor, all of which were locked and empty, Lily decided to call it a day, and give herself the day off. Marching out of the front entrance, Lily blinked in the brilliant blue sunshine that was draped over the street like a dazzling blanket, and set off for home.

The area still seemed strangely quiet, bearing in mind it was now after 9 am; Lily passed a man walking on the other side of the road, who looked at her quickly, then seemed to do a double-take just after he'd gone past. Lily could feel his eyes burning a hole into the back of her head, and couldn't resist a quick peek round to see what he was doing. The man was looking at Lily with a strangely piercing stare, and a smile that didn't seem to reach his lips.

Lily stared at him for around ten seconds, before dismissing him as some sort of perverted loon, and walked on. There was no reason for the man to stare the way he had; she hadn't suddenly grown three heads. Her long auburn curly hair was hanging around her pretty, make-up encrusted face the way it always did; she was dressed like any other female student, in a purple sweater, short skirt, purple tights, black ankle boots, and a large brown jacket, topped off with a scarf and hat. Nothing out of the ordinary - unless the man was some kind of psychotic crackpot who hated women..

As she neared the opening of Carpenter Street, Lily spotted a large, brown and black striped cat that was licking itself with enthusiasm. Lily diverted slightly to pat the creature on it's furry black head. The cat stopped it's ablutions and moved to rub it's head and back against Lily's legs, with a contented purr. As she bent to stroke the cat's arched back, Lily realised with a start that the cat had only three legs; but the missing leg didn't seem to be missing due to some amputation-inducing accident. Rather, the cat seemed to be perfectly comfortable with it's three limbs, two of which were the expected hind legs, the third was situated at the creature's midriff. Lily noted that the cat didn't move in the expected `hopping' way that having three legs might suggest; instead it seemed to glide forwards and backwards, all the while purring contentedly as Lily stroked it's arching brown back.

As Lily patted the cat one last time, and prepared to move on she looked up and with a shock of startled disbelief mixed with terror, saw the man who had been staring at her before. He was stood just ten feet away, and was staring at her in open revulsion and fear; Lily quickly set off half-walking and half-running in the direction of home. She passed more people on the way, and to her surprise, they all stared at her in mingled fear and disgust the exact same way that the man had, the man who was half-walking, half-running after her.

By now, Lily was being pursued (there was no other word for it) by a crowd of about twenty people. She wanted to scream at them in outrage and anger, but was getting out of breath. Finally, within seven feet of her front door, she tripped and fell headlong into the road. She wasn't hurt at all, just slightly dazed, and desperate to get away from the crowd of loonies who had stopped running and just stood now, in a large group. The crowd was looking intently at the quietly terrified Lily, who had gotten to her feet and was looking at them in mute appeal to explain themselves. The man who had been the first to stare was at the front of the group; he looked at Lily, then yelled "FREAK!!" with such utter hatred and passion that Lily turned white.

The man then turned around slowly in the direction of the crowd. Lily saw that situated right in the middle of the back of his head was a third eye, visible through the hair that surrounded it on all sides, that seemed to be staring at her intently. Several minutes later, and the crowd stood over the dead, bludgeoned body of Lily Stewart, looking down at her with a mixture of incredulity and disgust.

Shot at Dawn

Shot At Dawn

by Jamie Tucknutt

It was approaching 6am on a cold, damp morning in an otherwise nondescript field at the Somme in late September of 1916. It was misty and still. The stillness, no doubt, in total contrast to what must have been the madly pounding hearts of the two young men of the Northumberland Fusiliers tied to rough wooden posts and facing the twelve of their comrades who made up the firing squad. Men of their own Company. Men who they had fought alongside and indeed some of whom they knew from their lives in Newcastle and the surrounding areas before the War.

Sgt Cornelius Andrews, a career soldier in his late 30s, was in charge of the firing squad. Not that he took any pride whatsoever in his task. He was enough of a soldier to know it was utterly wrong to be shooting his own men. Men! They were barely out of their teens. Lord Kitchener's New Army had served up a never ending supply of kids to be slaughtered in the fields. While not a religious man, Sgt Andrews had discussed this onerous task with the Padre and decided that he was going to get it over with as quickly and as practically as possible. Both for the benefit of the men being executed and their fellow soldiers standing witness. You see the Army felt it character-building and likely to discourage such behaviour if they forced to stand on parade and watch the shooting.

One of the witnesses to this particular execution was a tall, gangling Private called Godfrey (Goff) Wood who had lied about his age to the recruiting Sergeant in order to join up and seek action & adventure. Pretty quickly after arriving at he front however, Goff had began to rue his decision. Even more than the industrial scale slaughter he had seen so far, this absolute travesty of 'justice' was making him curse that afternoon on Newcastle Town Moor when in a spirit of youthful exuberance and thrill-seeking he had joined the long line of men queuing to sign up for the Army and fight for King and Country.

Sgt Andrews was carrying a pistol as it was his duty to deliver the coup de grace in the event either condemned man survived the firing squad. His orders were to dispatch the wounded man with a shot to the head from point blank range. "Dear God, I know I'm not much of a one for prayers but please make sure I don't have to use this," he whispered to himself as he rechecked that it was fully loaded before issuing the orders to all present. He called the witnessing party and the two prisoners to attention and read out the charges. "Private Thomas Nash, you have been court-martialled and found guilty of desertion and cowardice in the face of the enemy. Private William Swinburne, you have been court-martialled and found guilty of desertion in the face of the enemy. You are both sentenced to death by firing squad the sentence having been confirmed by Field Marshall Haig. Do either of you have anything you

wish to say?" Contrary to popular belief the condemned man was not given a final cigarette, just a chance to say a few words before being shot and then hastily buried as if to cover up the shame and forget about it. Private Nash was only 19 years old and was too far gone emotionally and psychologically to register anything other than his impending death, he trembled uncontrollably and closed his eyes to resign himself to his fate. Private Swinburne, also 19, whispered a just about audible, "Mother" and burst into tears.
Sgt Andrews gave the command "Ready," and raised his right arm vertically, at which the firing squad unlocked their rifles. ""'Aim," and a lowering of his right arm to the horizontal, signalled to the firing squad to take aim at the white paper targets pinned over each man's heart and finally "Fire" and Sgt Andrews dropping his arm directly to his side was met with a loud 'crack' as all twelve rifles fired simultaneously.
Goff winced and wondered, indeed hoped, that someone else in the witnessing party was feeling as sick to their stomach as he was. Captain Kingsley-Fisher and the medical officer, Surgeon Lieutenant Manley walked over to where the two executed men were slumped awkwardly against the posts, only held in a vaguely upright position by their bindings. Lt. Manley checked both pulses and confirmed they were dead. Sgt Andrews felt a brief surge of relief that he wouldn't be called on to finish the job, then guiltily reprimanded himself for thinking of his own feelings when two of his men had just been killed.
That afternoon, Goff wrote home to his sister Mary. He told her of the executions and how unbelievably stupid it was shooting our own men during a war. Surely that was the job of the Hun, he suggested. He asked how everyone was and then suggested she knit him some thick socks what with winter being on the way. Goff and his sister had always been close despite Mary being eight years older than him. She was married with her own child now and had begged Goff not to join up as soon as she had heard he was thinking of doing so and told him that, as a mother, she knew just how worried their own Mam would be. Goff posted the letter then went for a cup of tea and some banter with the lads.

The next morning, Sgt Andrews came up to Goff looking more than a little concerned. 'Slinger lad," he said [in the armed forces certain surnames guarantee a particular nickname will be allocated to you; Smudger Smith, Chalky White, Shady Lane etc. For some reason, those with the name Wood have always been Slinger], "I don't know what you've done but Captain Kingsley-Fisher wants to see you right now. Most insistent he was that I fetch you personally. Best straighten yourself up and look lively fella. It won't pay to keep the officer waiting."
"Any idea what it's about Sarge?" asked Goff. He'd been afraid of being found out as being an underage soldier ever since he had sailed from England and had

gone out of his way to fit quietly in without putting his head above the parapet [pun intended].
"Who do you think I am, lad, Gypsy Rose Lee and her crystal ball?" Sgt Andrews laughed and he gave Goff a playful kick up the backside. "Just move your skinny arse and find out. Maybe you're going to be granted a week's leave back home for being Soldier of the Month!"
Goff dashed to the Officers' Quarters as quickly as he could whilst also racking his brains for the reason he had been summoned. No one ever got sent for personally by the Captain, certainly not a humble Private.
Lieutenant Grenville-Harcus was loitering around as near to the Captain as he could. "No change there then the arse-kisser, thought Goff. "Private Wood," he said in his usual condescending manner, "Wouldn't like to be in your boots, old chap. The Captain seems in a frightful mood. Better go straight in," and he ushered Godfrey through to the Captain's doorway and announced his arrival.
"Thank you Lieutenant," said the Captain as he motioned for Grenville-Harcus to leave them and close the door. "Come in Wood." Goff just about managed to make it in front of the Captain's table on very shaky legs, he stood to attention and saluted. The Captain saluted back and started, "Well Wood, you've made a decent fist of this soldiering so far, received good reports from your platoon and from Sgt Andrews, which is why it pains me so that it should come to this," and at that he produced the letter that Goff had wrote to his sister just the previous day. He placed it on his table in front of them so he could read the contents he had written. "Censor says he damn near had a heart attack when he read it. Got it sent to me straight away. What the hell were you thinking Wood?"
Goff looked at he letter and saw, circled in bold pencil, his words 'of the many stupid things I have seen since I got here, none were more stupid than watching, in fact being forced to watch, two of my mates being filled with bullets by our own men'. "I see you reading the offending item Wood," said the Captain sternly, "And it continues in much the same vein right through to the end. Almost sounds like it was written by a damned conchie. They were shot for desertion and cowardice Wood. Very, very serious charges in wartime. You see, that sort of thing can spread very quickly and very easily. Hence why we must come down hard on them. Now double away smartly and write your sister a proper letter. Tell her how good morale is. Yours and that of your comrades. Tell her how proud you all are to be serving King and Country and how you hope to be home by Christmas. No more of this lily-livered stuff Wood, I'm told you're a better soldier than that. Dismissed." Goff saluted, did an about turn and doubled out of the room straight into Lt Grenville-Harcus, almost bundling him over.
"Sorry sir,' said Goff, thinking to himself that's what you get for listening in at doors you little creep, "Didn't see you there."

"Hope for your sake you aren't going coward on us Wood," sneered Grenville-Harcus, "I wouldn't have the slightest hesitation in recommending you be shot. Plenty more where you came from to step up and take your place." Goff was a little taken aback, briefly considered how pleasing it would be to punch the little squirt, then dashed off back to his billet. He was hoping to get a little shut-eye before being on night duty later.

Usually, night duty in the forward trench consisted of looking out for German raiding or wire-cutting parties whilst also avoiding the occasional sniper fire should you be foolhardy enough to raise your head above the level of the trench. And never, ever be the third man to light your cigarette from a match; the initial flare of the match striking and lighting the first cigarette alerts the sniper, the second one lit allows him to get a good sighting, then the third gets his brains blown all over the other two. But tonight's was different. The artillery on both sides were going at it absolutely hammer and tongs, the Earth wasn't just shaking, it was positively bouncing with the impact of all the explosions. From what Goff could make out, shells were simply landing in pre-existing, blasted out shell holes, throwing tons of mud and debris into the air in order to create newer, bigger shell holes. Net gain = zero. In the rare event of a direct hit, men were simply vaporised and sprayed over huge areas and covering everyone around in a fine, red mist known to the soldiers as 'wet dust'. Goff looked out thinking that tomorrow was going to be another one of those days when they have to re-bury the dead as their graves had been blown up, yet again. Just another thing to add to the list of the absurdities of war.
"I think both us and the Hun must have got a load of shells as an early Christmas present, Slinger," said Sgt Andrews, breaking Goff out of his contemplation.
"Yes, Sarge. Looks that way doesn't it?"
Sgt Andrews laughed and continued, "Mark my words though, this time next week we'll be crying out for ammunition. The cloud-busters in the Royal Artillery have never been very good at rationing it out, I think they just like to make a loud noise to remind us all that they are still here. I shouldn't take to heart what the Captain said today, or was it yesterday. Yep, definitely yesterday'" he said after checking his watch.
"No Sarge?" Goff asked.
"Not at all. Everyone makes mistakes writing letters from time to time. Censors get very twitchy about us sounding war-weary or giving secrets away. Ha, not there are any secrets. I think both sides have made it pretty clear that their only plan is to throw men and munitions forwards until one side runs out thus determining a winner." Goff sniggered, he never suspected that the Sergeant thought way about the war, him being a professional soldier and all.
"How old are you Slinger?"

"Seventeen Sarge," he replied, just a little too quickly and enthusiastically. A raised eyebrow was all that it took to tell Goff that he hadn't been believed.
"Ok, fifteen really Sarge," he admitted, "But you wont tell anyone will you? I want to earn my home leave the same way as everyone else."
"Listen son, I knew you was underage. But 15, bloody hell. No, I wont say anything. You had your reasons for coming out here in the first place and its not for me to get you sent back. To be honest, I don't think they'd send you back anyway. As you've no doubt seen, we need all the men we can get."
"Which is why I found it so stupid to be shooting our own men," Goff said before he could stop himself.
"Ha! You'll get no argument from me there son. Just be careful who you voice your opinions in front of."
"You mean like Lieutenant Grenville-Harcus?" Godfrey suggested, "He told me he'd have no hesitation in ordering me to be shot if he thought I was a coward."
"He did, did he lad?" mused Sgt Andrews, "I shouldn't pay too much attention to anything the Lieutenant says. You see he's from a long line of decorated army officers. I'll bet some of them were so brave they were almost close enough to see the actual fighting!" Goff laughed out aloud, Sgt Andrews continued,"And he's just desperately trying to get a chestful of medals to be among them in the family history. He doesn't care how many other men's lives it costs him to achieve it. Just you bear that in mind Slinger." Goff was just about to thank the Sergeant for for putting his mind at rest when they heard a blood-curdling scream coming from the German trench less than 100 yards from where they stood.
"That sounded like a man being sent to meet his maker in a very painful way," said Sgt Andrews, "I didn't know we had a raiding party out."
"We haven't Sarge."
"Well it definitely was not a happy man. So unless one of the Hun has got a 'Dear John' letter from his Fraulein, I'd say somebody just got killed." Keep your eyes peeled Slinger, I'll do a quick check of all of our sentries and ask if they've seen or heard anything." With that Sgt Andrews melted into the darkness the way only a professional soldier or silent assassin can. Goff strained his eyes to scour the desolate wastes of no-mans land for any movement. Though limited in experience, Goff felt it sounded like a man whose nerve had betrayed him. He'd seen a man with Trench Fever (or Shellshock now known to be PTSD) only a month or so ago. Previously a very good soldier, the man had quickly become a gibberish-gabbling and trembling shadow of his former self. Unable to speak, or even attempt to make himself understood, he'd even wet himself as medics tried to care for him. Goff found it hugely unnerving to see. Sgt Andrews came back after about half an hour looking more than a little perplexed, "Moore has gone. I'm not sure if he's AWOL, I personally doubt it, or maybe that was his scream we heard earlier."

“No Sarge, that was definitely from the German trench. More or less directly opposite from me.’
“In that case Slinger, it looks like we’ve just had another deserter. I’ll go and cover that position till morning, we cant leave that flank uncovered,” and Sgt Andrews disappeared for a second time. Bloody hell, thought Goff to himself, that’ll be another one for a firing squad once he’s caught.
However, Private Anthony Moore wasn’t for the firing squad. He was found at more or less first light not 20 yards away from his night sentry post. Or, rather, what was left of him was found. He had been disembowelled, with numerous organs missing and his brain had been removed as neatly as if someone had cut the top off a boiled egg at the breakfast table. Goff heard the soldiers discussing it as he tried to get some sleep. “Filthy Hun,” said one voice. “War is war but that was just murder, sadistic murder,” added another.

The thing was, it wasn’t a ‘filthy hun’ that had committed these overnight atrocities. Over in the German trenches an equally horrific scenario had been discovered at first light. Three soldiers who had been on night duty were found murdered in eerily similar circumstances. Each had been cut wide open with organs either missing, or so strewn around the area it was impossible to tell whose was whose. One had been decapitated, of his head there was no sign, and left hanging on the barbed wire, arms spread out, in something akin to a mock-crucifixion.
“English dogs,” uttered one of the onlookers with disgust, “They must pay for this. This is not was, this is just savagery. They are worse than animals.”

Goff was intrigued by the snippets of conversation he’d heard. Too intrigued to get back to sleep, he got up and went to help himself to a cup of tea. After filling his tin mug from the communal, ever-present pot, Goff joined a group of soldiers who were discussing the killing of Private Moore and the mess that had been made of his body. He told them he’d heard screams coming from the German reaches when he’d been on duty last night.
“Are you sure the scream was from the Germans?” one soldier asked him, “Only we reckoned it might be some sort of scare tactic by them on a raiding patrol to unnerve us.”
“It bloody unnerved me,” said another, “Tony was done up like a Jack the Ripper victim. I seen him with my own eyes. Blood and guts everywhere. And his head...” the soldier stopped, looking sick to his stomach at the memory.
“It was definitely from their trench I heard the screams. Almost directly opposite my post,” Goff replied, “Even Sgt Andrews heard it and agreed with me where it was coming from. At first we reckoned it was one of our raiding parties, only we didn’t have any out. I wonder if there’s a madman on their side

came across and did for poor Tony then went back over and attacked his own men."
"Maybe the madman is from our side!" chipped in one of the group, causing them all to stop and think awhile.

Two weeks went by, two fairly uneventful weeks. Well, as uneventful as can be expected in the trenches of World War 1. Just the usual shelling, gas attacks, machine gunfire and the occasional sniper blowing someone's head off when they inadvertently failed to keep low at all times. There were no more blood-curdling nighttime screams or unexplained, horrific murders and talk of the killing of Private Moore was beginning to wane. The generally accepted opinion was that it had been a German soldier gone rogue in both sets of trenches and had been caught and executed. Goff was on a raiding party this particular night and was understandably nervous.
Raiding parties had to cross no man's land in total darkness and with total silence. The slightest noise heard by enemy sentries would mean flares being sent up, machine guns barking and the party being cut to pieces. Getting across no man's land was merely the beginning. Once there, they had to engage in the most medieval hand to hand trench combat, often against superior numbers. The aim was to destroy machinery and weapons, kill enemy soldiers and ideally return with maps, charts, plans and possibly even a prisoner or two to interrogate. Walking around the men, getting the odd "good luck young un" from those who weren't going, Goff could see who the old hands were at raiding parties. They relied less on standard army issue weapons, and more on their own handmade, job-specific creations. He saw spiked metal gauntlets, double headed hand axes and various other tools designed to inflict the maximum possible damage to the human body. All artfully built from artillery shell casings and any pieces of available scrap metal. One of them gave him a set of brass knuckledusters with spikes and blades added saying, "Here son, these have been useful to a few of the lads." Even by the usual standards, Goff thought, this was going to be brutal.
Night had fallen and the raiding party were assembled in the forward most trench, silent, their faces smeared in mud and carrying only the bare minimum of equipment. They were to be led by
Lt Charles and Sgt Peters, two solid blokes who were always good to have on your side. It was the Sergeant who issued the 'team talk' prior to setting off. "Right lads," he whispered, "for those who haven't been out on a raid before, and also a reminder for those of you who have, keep low, move slow, use the terrain for cover. When using wire cutters, make it nice and smooth so you make as little noise as possible when the tension gives in the wire. If a flare does go up, the temptation is to drop or look for cover. Don't. Stay perfectly

still. Movement is the giveaway. Alright? Put your fags out now. Best of luck everyone."
Climbing over the top, flat on his stomach, Goff feared for an instant his courage would betray him but he took a deep breath and slid over. He quickly took in the layout of the ground before him to plan his route with as much cover as possible. Nods, gestures and hand signals between all members of the party were the only types of communication they dared to use. But using these, and what seemed like plenty of luck as far as being spotted or heard was concerned, they made good time across no mans land.
Pretty soon, they were almost upon the Germans. Sgt Peters looked a little perplexed, as did Lt Charles. There was no sound or sign of movement from the trench not ten feet in front of them. Peters gathered them into a group just behind the last mound of earth. He joked in a whisper that the German sentries must be asleep and primed everyone to be ready to leap into the trench. He said they would try for two prisoners at most, the rest were to be killed.
On Lt. Charles's signal, Goff and all of his fellow raiding party leapt into the German trench ready to confront the nearest German and then stab, club or otherwise subdue them as swiftly and as silently as possible. But instantly they realised that someone had beaten the to it. Save for one wide-eyed individual sat on the ground with his back to the wall and shaking uncontrollably, they were already dead. Not just dead. But dismembered, decapitated and disembowelled with body parts strewn all over so it was difficult to tell where one man ended and the next one began. Goff and another soldier grabbed the surviving German and he gave no struggle whatsoever. In fact, he appeared to be overwhelmed with relief and was more than happy to be taken prisoner by the British. He grabbed Goff's arm tightly and babbled incoherently.
Sgt Peters looked shocked and horrified and Goff suspected that it was the first time for a long while. He just about kept his voice steady and managed to say, "Time we were going back now fellas. There's nothing and no one here for us except this prisoner and he's making enough noise to rouse the rest of them. Homeward bound."
Back in the relative 'safety' of home trenches Goff's main problem, other than trying to disengage himself from the German who held on with both hands and showed no sings of letting go, was preventing the majority of the Tommies from wanting to shoot the prisoner on the spot.
"He's murdered his own just like he murdered Tony Moore," they had deduced.
"But look at him," Goff said, still trying to at least get the German to loosen his grip slightly, "he's skinnier than me. How could he have overpowered big Tony Moore and killed him that way. And there were about eight dead Germans in the trench beside him just now, torn apart. No way is he a murderer." A few looked swayed by Goff's argument but still one or two were not.

“They say a madman has the strength of ten. Listen to him, he’s not making any sense he must be mad,” one Tommy said, his rifle still pointed at the German.
“Steady lads,” came the voice of Sgt Andrews, much to Goff’s relief, “no one is shooting anyone until we’ve interrogated this prisoner. Everyone get some sleep now and we’ll look at this with fresh eyes in the morning. Maybe it’ll make a bit more sense then, because it makes bugger all right now.” There were mutters and mumblings but everyone respected the Sgt too much to try to argue and so they sloped off to grab a few hours sleep. “You too Slinger,” he said to Goff, then as he managed to get the German to let go, “you come with me Fritz. I’m locking you up but you’ll be safe. We’ll have a talk in the morning.”
After a couple of hours not exactly sleep, but at least a sort of rest and a cup of tea, Goff reassembled with the previous night’s raiding party for a debrief. He took a little personal satisfaction in noting that the other far more experienced soldiers, including Sgt Peters and Lt Clark, looked as pale, bewildered and sleepless as he felt. Every man had an equal say and in such unprecedented circumstances as they had all endured, all were told they could say exactly what they saw, heard or felt. Nothing was off limits, “Though, of course, the actual report we hand in will be sanitised,” said Lt Charles, drily. To a man they came to the conclusion that their prisoner was neither the killer of his own colleagues last night, nor the killer of Private Moore previously. In this open minded atmosphere Goff felt less stupid than he otherwise would have done telling them that the prisoner, whose name was Ralf, said some creature had risen up from the ground and killed his friends before flying off.
“He tried to describe it sir,” Goff said, “but my German isn't great and he was far too out of it to make any sense. I know it sounds daft but he said it had tentacles as well as wings and that it spoke to him about the old gods and something that sounded like Nyarlathotep. He couldn’t translate that and said it isn't German.
“Shellshock sergeant?” suggested Lt Clark.
“Possibly sir. Or maybe just stark terror after seeing one of his comrades run amok killing all around him. Either way it'll be tough to get anything meaningful from him in interrogation. Though I hear this time Lt Stewart-Short has asked personally if he can do the questioning. He’s the best man for getting inside the head of a crazy.”
“Quite,” laughed Lt Clark, “possibly because he’s three quarters of the way there himself.”
Lt Stewart-Short was indeed the best man for the job, and not just because of his psychiatric training and the fact he spoke fluent German. No, he also happened to have studied in Maine, USA before the war and was therefore, as an extremely lucky consequence, particularly well-versed in Cthulhu Mythos. The instant he had seen the word ‘Nyarlathotep’ in the notes regarding the ill-fated trench raiding party, he had been determined to make the case his own. He

set off as soon as possible and managed to arrive around lunchtime and was straight away introduced to Goff, who had gained the trust of the prisoner, Ralf, and Sgt Andrews who would assist in the interrogation from a military intelligence perspective.
All three of them entered a ramshackle outbuilding that was doubling up as a cellblock. Ralf was sat on the floor in a corner, bound hand and foot and muttering to himself. "He's been doing that all night sir," said the sentry, glad to be relieved of his duty of guarding the scary prisoner, "mostly German, but sometimes this language I've never heard before. Sounds like he's talking to the Devil himself."
Lt Stewart-Short gave a wry grin, "You may not be a million miles from the truth there Private. Go and get some grub and then get your head down lad, we'll be here a while."
"Thank you sir," said the sentry and departed rather quickly looking over his shoulder as he did so. Ralf brightened visibly upon seeing Goff. Lt Stewart-Short asked Sgt Andrews to untie the prisoner and motioned them all to sit in a close circle so as to create a less intimidating atmosphere.
"Sergeant," he said, "I'm aware we are supposed to be interrogating the prisoner for matters of military intelligence and security. But as we can see, its unlikely at the moment that we could put much faith in anything he told us. I'd like to start therefore, by asking about the other matters first. The so-called elephant in the room as it were."
"He never said it was an elephant sir," protested Goff, "he just said it had tentacles. More like an octopus than an elephant."
"No Private," laughed Lt Stewart-Short, "the elephant in the room just means a big, overarching topic that we are all aware of and should be talking about but everyone deliberately avoids for one reason or another."
"Oh, sorry sir," Goff mumbled reddening in the face.
"No problem lad, Goff is it?"
"Yes sir."
"Ok, you two fellas just call me Shorty while it's just us around. Can't stand all of this ranks and saluting rubbish. I want to get Ralf here to get off his chest what he saw last night. Firstly, because it really intrigues me and secondly, once we've got him at ease he may be able to give us a little more accurate military information. That sound alright?"
"Fine by me sir. Erm Shorty," said Sgt Andrews, "young Slinger here has already told me the poor chap is almost insane so I'm prepared to go slowly and follow your lead."
"Thank you Sgt," said Shorty, then turning to Ralf and speaking to him in German, "now young man, I appreciate you've had a terrific shock and may even be doubting yourself as to whether you saw the things you did. But let me tell you now, I will believe you. No matter how unlikely you think the story

sounds. I want you to tell me in your own words, exactly what happened in your trench last night before the British soldiers arrived."
Ralf, though still thoroughly shaken, was somewhat calmed by the voice of Shorty and gathered his thoughts, "I was talking to two friends. There were several others around too. I turned to make coffee for us…"
"Go on."
"Then the ground came alive beneath their feet. A creature sir. Made from mud. The earth we were standing on. It just rose up to about two or three metres tall and had thick tentacles. These tentacles just tore them men apart like rag dolls. But it spoke sir, it spoke to me."
"Yes Ralf, I'm told you can repeat what it said."
"I couldn't make out all of what was said. I think I was screaming constantly. But it said Nyarlathotep several times, and crawling chaos and something about the elder gods awakening. I know this sounds insane but when I close my eyes I can still see it clearly and remember its voice. I know what I saw and I know what I heard."
"What do you think sir?' asked Sgt Andrews, "I know we agreed to believe everything he tells us, but this does seem a case of shellshock wouldn't you say?'
"I believe him," said Goff outright, "my grandfather was a miner and he used to tell stories about what he and his mates had seen and heard underground. I think we put it down to miners' folklore at the time, but this is making me think maybe there was something in his tales. And don't forget the state of those bodies last night. Nothing human could've done that.
Shorty spoke briefly to Ralf, then turned to Goff and Sgt Andrews, "Let me tell you men. This is not folklore, nor is it shellshock. I don't suppose either of you are familiar with Cthulhu and the Elder Gods?" Two utterly blank faces indicated indicated that he was right in his assumption so he continued, "this creature he speaks of, Nyarlathotep. It is a winged and tentacled creature and a member of the gods of which Cthulhu is the most powerful. These old gods lived here before us, before the dinosaurs even. It is said they lie sleeping underground, under the sea bed and even under the North and South poles waiting for the right time to awaken. I would guess that millions of tons of bombs and shells detonating on the earth's surface may hasten that awakening."
Sgt Andrews let out a whistle then announced, "I'm from farming stock in Cornwall, where the piskies live, so I already believe there are creatures living on this earth of which we have no knowledge. But I would warn you that we'd better be very careful how we talk about this and who we talk about it to. We don't want to be shot for faking insanity in order to get back to Blighty."
"Agreed Sergeant," said Shorty, "we'd also better ensure he is closely guarded at all times. More for his own safety than for security. The Elder Gods may think he's our best chance at a link between our world and theirs."

“Right you are. I’ll organise the guard roster. Slinger, I’ll put you and me down for as many nights as possible. He seems to feel safer around you plus I think he’s give most men the heebie-geebies with his gabbling in tongues and his staring eyes.”
Goff was something of a hero among his pals in the trenches due to his exploits the night before despite him playing it all down. “Well done young un” and “have a cigarette mate,” rang in his ears wherever he went. He even had a mug of tea brought to him while they asked him about what had happened. He could've played up his role a bit, but Goff was honest enough to tell them that no, he hadn’t had to subdue the prisoner and also no, he hadn’t actually seen anything or anyone other than all of the dismembered German bodies in the trench. After a while the conversation got back round to the usual topics of letters from home (or lack thereof), food (and both the lack and the poor standard of) and leave (the impossibility of obtaining). But then the relative peace was suddenly shattered.

An unearthly, scream followed by an extended, and equally-spine chilling howl brought everyone and everything to a standstill. Bewildered men looked at each other thinking, has the murderer struck again? But surely nothing human could've made a noise like that. Emphasising the potentially supernatural aspect, the sky suddenly darkened, turning a purplish-black in colour. As if evil itself had descended. Thunder rumbled long and loud and a hailstorm broke. Instinctively Shorty knew what was occurring, or at least who was involved. He dashed out of the officers’ dug out and headed straight for the makeshift cellblock. Goff saw him run by and followed hot on his heels, “Sgt Andrews,” he shouted, “Sgt Andrews. Ralf. The prisoner.” The Sergeant picked up his rifle and ran with them. On reaching the cellblock they saw Lt Grenville-Harcus barking instructions to the two sentries.
“What the hell have you done?’ Shorty shouted as he pushed past the three of them and into the open cell door.
There, on the floor, still tied at hands and feet, was the body of Ralf. He had been shot in the head, no doubt by Grenville-Harcus’s pistol which he was still holding. Goff and Sgt Andrews stood behind Shorty looking on in disbelief as Ralf’s body twisted and contorted like some writhing snake.
Goff made to rush forward, “He’s still alive-” but Shorty quickly flung out an arm to block his path.
“I’m afraid not. The human is dead and the creature dwelling within is in its death throes. It’s a shape-shifter and goes through all of the forms and identities it has ever taken upon its death.”
Appalled though they were, Goff and Sgt Andrews were unable to avert their unbelieving gaze. Ralf was totally unrecognisable, both as himself and as a

human being. He seemed to flow from one shape to another, none of them resembling anything living on Earth."
Meanwhile Shorty grabbed Grenville-Harcus by the arms and slammed him into the wall, "Do you know what you've done you ignorant fool?" he shouted.
"He was diseased. It must've been a brain disorder. I killed him before he could kill again. He's the murderer," he whined pitifully.
Shorty took Grenville-Harcus's face in his left hand and forcibly turned his head to make him watch the unfolding horror. "Does this look like a brain disorder? You've lost us our one link with what is happening here," he let go and Grenville-Harcus collapsed to knees before vomiting at the sight, "we've got no means of communicating with Nyarlathotep now until he returns. And he will. Far from preventing further killing, you've just written a death warrant for more men. Possibly all of us. Now get out of my sight."
Ralf, and the creature inhabiting his body, were dead. As such, his body was back in human form. Sgt Andrews suggested they bury him and explain the gunshot wounds by stating he was killed whilst attempting to escape. He added, "I hate to cover for that idiot Grenville-Harcus but it's the best way of keeping a lid on things."
Shorty adopted a wry grin, "For now that is Sergeant. I've a feeling everyone will know the truth when Nyarlathotep returns."

Shorty successfully persuaded the top brass at HQ that he should stay on to further interrogate the prisoner, his real motive however was to ensure he was there when Nyarlathotep returned. He wanted to meet the creature/god/demon and, if he survived, try to communicate with it. His long term plan was to devise a way to kill it or failing that, send it back from whence it came.
But of course, the ebb and flow of the seemingly endless war being fought across no-mans-land stopped for nothing and no one. The higher echelons of both sides must have put any reports they did receive regarding the incident down to temporary insanity, mis-sightings, crossed wires in communications or even attempts to be recalled from the front on medical grounds. The British trenches especially took a heavy artillery pounding over the next two or three days. The men dug in as deep and as best as they could but kept a watchful eye open for the inevitable all-out assault that would surely follow the bombardment.
Sure enough, as one damp and misty dawn was breaking, the shelling stopped and minutes later a series of whistles punctuated the early morning quiet.
"Here they come lads," the shout went up. It looked to be a real concentrated effort this time as more Germans than usual were clambering up and into the fray. Their progress appeared to be all too smooth, no doubt helped by some earlier accurate shelling having put paid to the barbed wire defences of the British. Wave after wave of German soldiers just kept coming. A brave but

horrific scene, each felled soldier immediately has his place taken in a relentless assault. British machine guns rattled until the barrels were red hot and volley after volley of rifle fire was let loose but still the Germans advanced.
When suddenly, like a soundless explosion, the ground rose up and was flung all around just in front of the German troops. Nyarlathotep had returned in full fury. Standing fully ten feet tall with his powerful tentacles reaching out in all directions, he crushed, maimed and pulled apart men of both sides. Many of the nearby Germans simply recoiled in terror at the sight and were killed where they froze in position. Others turned tail and fled, while some, as well as some of the British soldiers who remained at their posts, concentrated their fire on the creature. It's loathsome, misshapen bulk, its thick, muscular tentacles, even its fragile looking, bat-like wings were impervious to bullets of any calibre. No amount of grenades thrown in its direction had no effect. Pretty soon the German attack was decimated or had fled. Nyarlathotep then half-slithered, half-crawled over the parapet and dropped into the British trench. Again, neither bullet nor bayonet troubled it in the slightest. As was its wont, it followed the line of the trenches raining death and chaos on all in its way.
Goff was cornered and so charged the creature with his bayonet. He leaned into the impact and put all of his strength behind it, twisting the bayonet to cause maximum damage. It felt like he was trying to pierce the toughest leather with a blunt shoemaker's needle. Nyarlathotep stood stock still as if mocking Goff by letting him try with all his might. It then circled his waist with a tentacle and lifted him off the ground. Goff dropped his rifle and thought that death was imminent. But Nyarlathotep spoke to him, whispering but still somehow being heard above the shouts of the men and the gunshots, "Ph'nglui mglw'nafh Cthulhu R'lyeh wgah'nagl fhtagn." [translated - in his house at R'lyeh, dead Cthulhu waits dreaming].
Nyarlathotep then simply melted away into the trench wall as if transformed into the very clay that made up the Somme battlefield.
Sgt Andrews was the first man to Goff who was sat on the ground with his eyes wildly staring at nothing in particular and a length of drool hanging from the corner of his mouth. "I'm sorry Slinger," he said, holding Goff tightly as if by doing so he could somehow resolve the problem. But, of course it was futile. Goff was still on this Earth in body, but his mind was now in other worlds, other dimensions. He was taken to the hospital where he sat harmlessly enough just endlessly repeating, " Ph'nglui mglw'nafh Cthulhu R'lyeh wgah'nagl fhtagn." It was several weeks before he was sent back home, and in all of that time it was a rare occasion that he uttered anything else. But when he did, he said in the clearest English, "Even death may die."
Goff's colleagues, most of whom had correctly deduced he was an underage soldier, were heartbroken. Sgt Andrews especially, he had taken Goff under his wing and had hoped to get him through the war in one piece and return him

home. Sadly this was not to be and Goff came back to these shores, like so many others both before and after him, with his mind shattered.

Epilogue

Sgt Cornelius Andrews survived the war and returned to his beloved wife Mavis and their beautiful Cornwall home where they raised three fine sons who, on their father's advice, avoided the military and stuck to farming. He never saw Goff again but to the end of his days he would occasionally find himself wondering what had happened to the skinny Geordie lad he'd done his best to look out for.

Lt Grenville-Harcus III was elected MP for Woking in the 1922 General Election. However, before he could take his seat in the Commons it was discovered he had been embroiled in a huge financial scandal. So on what would have been his big day, instead of going to the Houses of Parliament, he was led into the dock of Number 1 court in the Old Bailey. From there he was found guilty and taken to HMP Dartmoor for the next seven years.

Private Godfrey Andrews, on reaching Britain, spent approximately six months utterly failing to respond to treatment in The Royal London Hospital before being transferred to an insane asylum set deep in the highlands of Scotland. He lived there until 1927 when he was moved to Miskatonic University in Arkham, Massachusets where he spent the rest of his life aiding the studies of Professor Stewart-Short, Head of the Cthulhu Mythos Dept. Goff was in a secure, but very comfortable apartment and received numerous visits from his family. His condition improved a little and he was able to pursue his passions of reading and botanical art. The insight gained from studying him prevented The Elder Gods from returning. He died in 1972.

Shockwave

SHOCKWAVE
BY
DAVID BRILLIANCE

Paul Revere sat grimly astride his horse, as the animal raced along the moonlit roads just after midnight. At precisely ten minutes after midnight, a beam struck both rider and animal, and both vanished in an incandescent glow leaving no trace whatsoever that they had ever existed.

The beam in question had come from a space vessel that was hovering many millions of light years away, orbiting a smallish red planet in the Ophiucus system. The ship's Captain, one Zylus Qurtz had ordered the ship's weapons officer to fire, the target being a slightly smaller vessel that was approaching from the surface of the planet. The two races had been at war for several months, and Captain Qurtz had been ordered to make a strategic attack on the small planet that was used as a large weapon-manufacturing base for the enemy. The enemy vessel came close to Qurtz' ship, fired and then dove quickly to starboard. Qurtz had barely enough time to order a second weapon barrage, as his ship shuddered slightly beneath his hoofed feet.

The order to fire again was given, but this beam missed it's target by some margin, and went wildly off into the depths of space, eventually reaching a small blue and white planet in the Sol star system of the Milky Way galaxy. And it was this beam that zapped Paul Revere and his steed into nothingness, and Earth's future history into the proverbial cocked hat.

You see, the midnight ride of Paul Revere has entered the annals of Human history as one of those most distinguished of historical subjects - a Very Important Event. Paul Revere (b 1735; d 1818 - in the usual order of history) was an American Industrialist, slightly famous for, amongst other things, his profession as an engraver and silversmith. The most famous thing that Mr Revere is noted for is his April 1775 late night ride to alert the massing US forces of the Colonial militia of the approaching British troops prior to the first engagement of the American revolutionary war.

However, as a result of being scorched into nothingness by a zeltron beam fired from millions of light years away, the famous midnight ride of Paul Revere never happened. This in turn led to a very different landscape being created and played out on the unfortunate planet Earth.

As a result of the disintegration of both man and steed, the massed troops didn't get prior warning of the British incursion and, as a result of that, the first engagement of the Revolutionary war took a different turn, with a massacre of the American colonists that was said to be unequalled in it's ferocity and bloodshed. Consequently, Paul Revere went down in history as a turncoat and traitor, who betrayed his own people to the British. Revere's name was despised through the years that followed, and held up as an example of the worst type of scum. The American Revolutionary war led to several more wars that ravaged the face of the world in the decades to come, wars that most likely would not have come to pass if the normal flow of history had not been altered.

Time hangs on a slender thread, and it seemed as if that thread had snapped. By the time 1911 had rolled around, there was an ongoing first World War which had dragged itself through year after bloody year, with horrific casualties mounting up every day. This war had begun in July 1903, and would not come to an end any time soon. Civilians were almost non-existent now; anyone over the age of ten was drafted into the never-ending battle that had rocked the globe, and seen almost two-thirds of the world's population wiped out..

Martha Gillespie-Odenrank got up out of her ragged and uncomfortable bunk, and almost dropped onto the floor. She was exhausted after so many skirmishes with the enemy - and the enemy was Man. For as long as she could remember, she had been raised to believe that Man was an inferior species; simply there to help procreate and thus keep the line of Humanity going. Man had gotten above Himself in the last twenty or so years, and the Female of the species had finally (much like the proverbial worm) turned. Martha had been a Sergeant in the `war to end mankind' ,as it had become known, for two long years now; she had been involved in many glorious campaigns against the enemy, had been decorated twice, and had the women in her regiment looking up to her with a mixture of fear and admiration.
Martha heard footsteps behind her, and turned to see her equally-tired and dispirited second-in-command enter the room: "Morning Sir" said Hilda Travers, wearily.

The War to End Mankind came to a bloody and dispiriting end for both sides in March 1935, and it would take another twenty years for men and women to reach even just the first step of a reconciliation between the sexes. By the time June 1968 rolled around, the last great war was being taught in schoolrooms around the globe, and dramatised accounts were turning up on the relatively new mediums of late night television and cinema. But another great disaster for Humanity lay just around the corner, one that more-or-less coincided with the first faltering steps towards space travel and exploration - the first manned trip to the moon, which an excited world watched with bated breath in December 1974..

You see, Humanity had attracted attention to itself with that first manned space trip. The landing on the moon was such a success that it was followed by the end of the following year with trips to Mars and the hostile atmosphere of Venus. It was these trips, with small two-man/woman crews that had caught the attention of some of the myriad alien races out there in the vast inky blackness of the cosmos; some of these alien watchers had been content to just observe, but others had more hostile intentions. By the Summer of 1976, Earth was an occupied planet in more ways than one: the Frotam had invaded, and what was left of Humanity on Earth had been herded into vast slave labour camps, or taken to the Frotami home world for the same reason. The Frotam looked more-or-less Human but were generally seven feet tall in height (even the women and children) and had two silvery antennae emerging from the side of their necks. They were sadistic and malevolent, treating the inhabitants of the conquered world like cattle. Until one day, the worm turned.

Martin Girrand 111 sat hunched in the tunnels underneath the city, covered in grime, sweat and dust. He mopped the perspiration from his brow with a shaking hand, then turned to the fifteen other similarly bedraggled specimens lurking in the darkness. They looked at him expectantly but said nothing. This group had been holding secret meetings for some time now. They had covertly studied the enemy, sought out their weaknesses, and prepared a plan that, if successful, would lead to other revolts across the world, and see Earth back in the rightful hands of it's Human masters. The group were gathered underneath a street that led to a Frotam stronghold, one of millions around the globe. Here, the lanky aliens lived in luxury, dining on the best foods and drinks, all served up by their Human skivvies who, by contrast were forced to live in squalor. Martin and his team had managed to get their hands on two very valuable Frotam weapons, which could do a great deal of damage if used in the right place. Martin fingered the weapon, which resembled a small golden pistol, in his trouser holster. It was now or never. Martin stood up and raised his hands gingerly, slowly pushing at the manhole cover above his head. Once it had been moved aside, he grabbed both sides of the hole and with help from two of his comrades, heaved himself up and onto the street. Nobody about, as he expected. Good. The enemy HQ was several metres away. The rest of the group slowly and painfully climbed up onto the derelict street, and then quickly ran for cover. Those lanky Frotam bastards would soon get their comeuppance, thought Martin..

By the end of June 1977, Earth was once again in Human hands. The Frotami had been systematically slaughtered - that attack on the base in Somerset had inspired similar revolts around the world as word had spread. Soon, there were no more than fifty of the enemy aliens in existence on this planet, and they were rounded up and knifed, shot, eviscerated, blown to bits, beheaded and burnt in a very short time period. This sent a clear message to any aliens who might have similar ideas of invasion - Earth people would fight back!

The world got back to some semblance of order in the next few years, with technological achievements and scientific advancements being paramount on the list of necessary goals that were needed to get the planet fully back on it's feet. This in turn led to a new world order coming into existence, one that prized science and technology above the very people they were there to serve..

On a crisp Autumnal morning in September 1984, Alan Curtis got up out of bed, showered, half-listened to the usual propaganda on the radio and loudspeaker system as he ate his stodgy breakfast, then set off for work. His wife and son were still asleep. Alan worked in the offices of the Ministry of the People, making sure that the rulers' version of events was the one that was filtered down and relayed to the masses. The planet was once again at war, this time with an aggressive alien race of conquerors called the Slyth. The Slyth were basically large mounds of quivering pinkish jelly, with various appendages and one huge eye; they had openly declared war on the planet and this had led to Earth's first major push into the creation of warp-powered space vessels, designed to travel and fight in outer space. Alan sighed as he read the latest news regarding the Earth fleet's attempt to bring the ongoing battle to a quick end by taking the fight to the enemy homeworld - a small red planet in the Ophiucus sector. The battle was going badly for Earth forces, but as ever, he was required to spin the thread of defeat into a new yarn of optimism and victory..

The battle against the Slyth continued for far longer than anybody could have anticipated. Earth itself remained relatively untouched, as both Earth and Slyth forces endlessly parried in the black void of space close to the alien homeworld. Ship after ship was blown to bits, but for every ship that destroyed, six more were constructed in the enormous shipyards on Earth and on Earth's moon, and the endless battle recommenced with nary a pause.

Alan Curtis Jnr was a much respected Commander in the field. He had been involved in the ongoing war against the Slyth since 1993, had been decorated numerous times for valour over the years, and had the men in his command looking up to him with a mixture of fear and admiration. Curtis Jnr had not seen his home planet for six years - the ongoing battle against those jellified aliens had lasted for an interminable period of time, and had seen both sides get nowhere fast. Curtis Jnr had lost many of his men in the never-ending struggle against the Slyth, a battle that had raged for so long it had become meaningless, with both sides unsure any more as to why they were actually fighting at all.

This latest day had seen very little action, as the enemy seemed to be hiding. Until the moment when a Slyth vessel suddenly seemed to appear over the rim of a passing comet, and hurtled directly at Curtis Jnr's vessel.
The Human crew were slightly startled but too well-trained to not respond for long. Curtis Jnr hesitated for the briefest of seconds, then gave the order to fire. The Slyth ship seemed to hover for a moment, and for an equally brief second, it seemed to be in two places at once. Unfortunately, the Zeltron beam that fired from the missile cone at the front of Curtis Jnr's ship chose the wrong target - the beam passed harmlessly through the ghostly, almost after-image of the enemy vessel and continued travelling through space until, eventually, it reached the atmosphere of the blue and white planet that Curtis Jnr's ancestors had hailed from.

Craggee the Robot

Craggee the Robot

by Jamie Tucknutt

Craggee loved this island. He didn't know where he was, yet. But he worked out he was still on Earth, he just wasn't sure of the year. One thing he did know, was that this place was special. It had crystal clear blue sea around it, snow white sands and fabulous forests. He found so many interesting things on his walks to take back to a study he had set up in a cave. Shells, fossils, feathers and flowers all found a place in his collection.

Craggee was a robot, a science robot, from 35th century Earth. He'd read about many of the plants and creatures he came across on this island, but he'd never seen any of them for real before. They had all died out in the 28th century due to climate disasters along with mankind. He wasn't really called Craggee, but one of the things that robots had 'inherited' from their original creators, the humans, was their almost constant need to give each other nicknames. His serial number, emblazoned across his chest, was CRG33 hence Craggee.

Being a 35th century science robot, Craggee was in possession of a phenomenal memory bank full of historical, astronomical, scientific and mathematical information. The reason he'd ended up back in 21st century was that a wormhole experiment he'd been engaged on in his own time had suffered a problem and catapulted him through time. It could've been worse, thought Craggee and he happily made the island his home

His first morning on the island he'd been walking on the beach when he saw a large, greenish-grey lump on the sand. At first Craggee thought it was a rock, but then to his delight he realised it was a turtle. Being a friendly chap, he walked over and introduced himself.

"Hi, I'm Craggee," he said, "I'm a robot, I gather you are a turtle. Let me tell you that you are the first turtle I've ever met."

"Well isn't that a coincidence," came the reply, "you see, I'm Papa Turtle and I've never met a robot before. By the way, what is a robot?"

From that moment on, Craggee and the Turtle family who lived in the seas around the island became best friends. He also met splendidly-coloured parrots and a troop of chattering monkeys who lived in the forest.

Craggee knew from the maps and encyclopaedias in his massive brain that island was uninhabited and even undiscovered by humans. He thought it very sad that such a wondrous place would soon be covered by the rising sea level and no -one know it had even existed, let alone been able to appreciate its beauty. He was so concerned by this that he sat for a full day in his cave studying maps and reports of 19th and 20th century sea farers. From these he calculated that the island had less than a year before it was submerged forever. Craggee knew he had to act, and fast.

“My friends,” said Craggee as he opened the emergency meeting he’d called, “thank you all for coming at such short notice. I’m so glad you did as this island faces a crisis like never before. As the Turtle family will no doubt be able to confirm, not only is the sea becoming more polluted, but its level is rising. And very, very quickly.”
Papa Turtle nodded in agreement and, being a wise old reptile, had worked out just what Craggee was going to warn them about. “How long before the island disappears Craggee?” he asked.
“I’m certain of my calculations, and it’s definitely within the next year.” The parrots squawked, the monkeys shrieked and every other species present also expressed their shock at this news. The island had been their home for generations. As far back as their histories and folklore could go, it was always there.
Craggee waited for quiet and then laid out his plan. His communication and transmission systems weren’t strong enough to cross the 14 century time divide to enable him to contact his colleagues. He wished to tell them of his time and space co-ordinates and arrange for them to lift the whole island and surrounding sea and take it back to the 35th century where it could be preserved forever. But fortunately he’d worked out that if he partially dismantled himself, he could reuse some of the circuitry to build a super-transmitter.
“You’d do that for us?” asked Papa Turtle.
“Yes, of course. They’ll be able to replace my legs when they come to rescue us.”
“In that case Craggee,” said a visibly emotional Papa Turtle, “it would be my great honour to carry you about and be your legs from now on.” and he reached out a flipper to shake Craggee’s hand.
Though robots are supposedly incapable of emotions, Craggee felt his inner electronics go all warm and fuzzy for an instant. But then logic kicked back in and the work began.
The monkeys collected enough wood to not only make the tower for the transmitter but also a seat for Craggee that fit neatly onto Papa Turtle’s back. Craggee’s circuits were repurposed, along with some of the metal that made up his legs, and before long the work was complete. Everyone stood around and looked at it, proud of what they had achieved with some fabulous team work. Craggee typed out the message to be sent, containing the co-ordinates of the island and a breakdown of all forms of life on and around it so their needs could be catered for. “Now we sit back and wait,” he said.
As they waited Papa Turtle took Craggee on an underwater experience showing him the coral reef near to the island and all of the various species of life that depended upon it. Craggee was thrilled to see yet more sights he had only ever seen pictures of in his own time and though he loved it, he was somewhat saddened to know it would all be gone in just a few hundred years.

On returning back to the island Craggee saw that his message had been pinged back to him and was marked 'undelivered'. Earth's orbit was just too full of space junk to allow a fairly low-grade transmission through.
Craggee again took himself off to his cave for some serious thinking and high-pressure problem solving. The only way to overcome these difficulties was to create a satellite transmitter, put it into space, and have it send its message from there. Now the main obstacle to that plan was that on 21st century Earth, the only microchip powerful enough to do the job was his own brain. He'd need therefore to literally use his head! It would be sent up into orbit and act as the satellite transmitter.
Papa Turtle could supervise the work and follow the plans that Craggee was going to draw up, but the monkeys would need to do the manual work as they had greater dexterity. For a robot, Craggee got very emotional when discussing the plans with his friends Mama and Papa turtle.
"I would so love to have been here on the beach in Spring when your eggs hatched and all of the babies emerged from the sand and headed down to the sea for their first time. It must be a magical sight," he told them.
Mama Turtle, overcome with tears, managed to reach up to Craggee on his seat astride Papa Turtle and hugged him tightly, "You truly are a wondrous creature Craggee. How lucky am I? The first robot I've ever met and he just happens to be the greatest."
Eventually the dreaded day came. I will spare you the grim details, suffice to say the first part of the operation was successful. But it was a solemn moment as Craggee's head was sent into space. Even the forest fell silent, all of the creatures sparing a thought for Craggee and his supreme sacrifice.
The second part also went well. Craggee's scientist colleagues, having received the SOS message, despatched their ship with equipment, experts and a vast glass orb. They retrieved island, ocean and inhabitants and took them to the safety of the 35th century mere days before rising seas would have swallowed them for good. If you were living in the 35th century, you'd see that Earth has two moons now. The second being a beautiful glass sphere with blue ocean, tropical island and all of the descendants of the animals lucky enough to meet, and be saved by, Craggee.
As for Craggee himself, well he stayed here with us in the 21st century and if you look up into a clear night sky, you may just see a tiny speck of coloured lights floating around, discovering new and interesting things and often thinking of Mama and Papa Turtle and friends.

The Unhaunted Inn

THE UNHAUNTED INN
BY
DAVID BRILLIANCE

Charlie Farrington was driving along the dark and lonely road that he seemed to have been driving along for the last thirty days, by the time he caught sight of the welcoming lights from the windows of the Inn. He pulled his small, slightly grimy and battered Volvo over from the main road, and parked in the small car parking spot adjacent to the inn.

After several minutes, Charlie got out and locked the car, looking up at the sign hanging and swinging gently in the night-time breeze; strangely, though the sign had a painted image on it - of two ducks, with the dark shape of what appeared to be a hooded figure standing behind them in silhouette - there was no actual name. Charlie didn't ponder on this for long. In fact, he didn't ponder on it at all. Putting the car keys into his pocket, he headed towards the main door of the inn, checking his watch as he did so: 20.35.

Charlie opened the door of the Inn, and stepped through, and it was then that the smell hit him.. A smell of must, mixed with some unidentifiable odour.. Was it vomit? It was obvious that the place was run by someone who didn't put hygiene on the list as a high priority. Charlie walked into what was obviously the bar area - it was empty, save for a bored-looking barmaid stood absently cleaning drinking glasses with a grimy red and white tea towel. The barmaid looked up as Charlie entered, but her somewhat dazed and vacant expression didn't change; probably thinking about getting off shift and meeting her boyfriend for a night out at whatever passed as entertainment in this God-forsaken spot, thought Charlie.

"Hello. Have you a room for the night?", Charlie asked in a neutral tone. The barmaid replied in a dull monotone "Yes, sir". Charlie thought to himself "This is going to be difficult", as he surveyed the thick-looking creature stood at the bar; her brown curly shoulder-length hair framed an attractive face that was utterly devoid of interest or emotion. "How do they employ these people?" thought Charlie, "they should at least employ people who can pretend to be interested in the job they are doing".

It was while Charlie was thinking the last word of this, that a door at the side of the bar area opened and what he presumed to be the Landlord entered. The man was fat, with the reddish complexion and prominent nasal hairs that seem to be compulsory for gentlemen of the portly persuasion. The man looked quickly at the barmaid, with an expression that was almost a question; he then turned and, without the slightest hint of a smile or any other expression beyond boredom, asked: "What can we do for you sir?". Charlie repeated the question he had posed to the dim barmaid several minutes earlier. This time, as well as the affirmative answer that the girl had given, the landlord gestured to the door he had come through and said "This way, sir". Charlie turned to the girl, and said in a voice that dripped with mild sarcasm "Thank you for your help". The girl just looked at him.

The portly Landlord ushered Charlie into what was some sort of reception area. Charlie filled in some details in a shabby-looking register, then followed his host up the creaking stairs to the upper floor of the establishment. The place looked positively filthy, and the smell of what could only be described as a positively ripe fart hung in the air to such an extent that Charlie had to restrain himself from gagging. The Landlord said not a single word, as he stopped outside a brown wooden door, produced a key and quickly turned it in the lock. The door creaked open, the Landlord holding it open for his guest to step through.

Charlie entered the room slightly cautiously; there was no smell of Human flatulence in here, thank God! The Landlord followed him, and flicked a switch. Lights came on, and the room was illuminated in a quite inviting way that belied the general tone of unfriendliness that the place reeked of - as well as the literal reek of what smelt like someone had emptied their bowels after eating nothing but green vegetables for a month. The place looked dusty, and the cobwebs that hung from the corners of the ceiling did not inspire confidence in any way. Charlie turned and looked at his host, who was stood looking at him with an expression of very mild distaste; Charlie stared back for the merest hint of a second then said curtly "This will do nicely, thank you".

Several minutes later, and the Landlord had gone, leaving Charlie to unpack his modest suitcase. It was still early: 21.25, so Charlie decided to pay another visit to the vacant barmaid downstairs and have himself a tipple or two before retiring. The girl was still idly cleaning glasses and staring into space, as if catatonic when Charlie entered. He was not altogether surprised to see that he was the only patron in the place; the smell alone, if it was a regular occurrence, would be enough to put anyone off. The bar itself was what you might expect to see in any sort of `Ye Olde Country Inn', with about ten round tables arranged, with chairs beside them. There were pictures hanging on the walls, one of which depicted a man in the process of removing his breeches - it was a painting from another century, perhaps the sixteenth? - and about to immerse himself in a lake. Near the man were stood a group of Ducks, and a strange hooded shape. Charlie realised with a tinge of surprise that these were the same as on the sign of the Inn outside. This thought in turn prompted Charlie to ask, by way of intending to attempt conversation with the girl "What's the name of this Inn. It doesn't seem to have one on the sign outside".

The barmaid ignored this question completely, instead fixing her customer with the dead stare she'd had since Charlie first saw her, and asked "What can I get you sir?" in her customary flat and disinterested monotone. The blatant disregard for his query suddenly aroused a burst of anger in Charlie, but he managed to keep it in check, and muttered "Pint of Cider, please".

The barmaid poured the drink, and handed the glass over, before asking for the money in the same deadened voice. Charlie handed over a crisp tenner, and got the change back without a word from either party. As Charlie sat on the dark red bar stool and sipped his drink, he carefully avoided any eye contact with the girl, but he could see that she was looking at him; the slight absurdity of it all almost made him want to laugh.

Time passed, almost intolerably slowly; eventually, at a quarter past Ten, Charlie decided to call it a night, put his glass on the bar, and without looking at the girl (Charlie's peripheral vision told him that she'd remained looking at him the entire time he'd been there) said a curt "Goodnight" and headed for the door that led to the reception area, that lead to upstairs. The farty smell still lingered, and Charlie was glad to get to his room. It didn't take him long to get undressed, and soon he was lying in the slightly cold bed. He lay on his back, with his eyes fixed on the cobwebs slightly drifting on the ceiling. Eventually, he drifted off into a slumber that lasted for several hours; until, for no readily apparent reason, he awoke with a start. Checking his watch, Charlie saw that it was 2.45 in the morning. He must have been asleep for about four hours at least; cursing, Charlie was irritated by the fact that he would have to resign himself to the fact he probably would remain awake now.

Time passed; Charlie did everything he could to get to sleep but to no avail. He dragged himself from the bed, and into the nearby bathroom. This was the first time he had been in it, and the stench of human flatulence was worse than ever here. Charlie doubled over, retching violently. He had half a mind to go and get the Landlord out of bed, and demand an explanation for the unsavoury stink that permeated the place, as well as an explanation for why the staff were so damn surly and rude. Eventually, his face red from the strain of retching, Charlie decided that it was best not to cause a scene and to just try to get to sleep, and then get the Hell out of the place first thing in the morning. Muttering furiously to himself, Charlie struggled back into the bed. As before, he felt not the slightest bit tired; what to do to pass the hours until it was light?

It was while he was pondering on the routine the rest of the week would bring that he dropped off into a brief deep sleep. The sleep lasted barely ten minutes, before Charlie awoke with a bigger start than he had before - the smell of fart was now in the room and was almost overpowering! Charlie couldn't be bothered to get out of bed, and instead rolled over and buried his face in the pillow, where his nostrils might get some blessed relief from the almost unendurable stench that assailed him. Charlie wondered if the smell was actually some sort of Joke Shop Fart Cannister, and that the Landlord had sprayed it everywhere as part of some twisted prank? Good way to ruin your business, Charlie thought. He had a very low opinion of the Landlord, but surely he couldn't be so dense as to actively attempt to sabotage his own business.

It was several minutes later that Charlie suddenly started, with an almost literal jump. For some inexplicable and bizarre reason, he felt incredibly frightened. There was no reason for the feeling of outright fear that hung over him; true, the smell was enough to make a sane man weep, but there was no reason for Charlie to feel the wave of anxiety that was threatening to drown him. He turned over, and looked around the room. It was empty as before, but for some reason, the feeling of fear persisted, accompanied by a strong sensation that he was being watched. Charlie cursed himself for being a fool, turned onto his side and attempted to get some more sleep.

It was an undeniable period of time later when Charlie seemed to wake, with perspiration bursting out of every pore. As he turned onto his back, he was horrified to see that an enormous Duck was in the room, waddling slowly towards him. Charlie couldn't believe the evidence of his own eyes, but he felt most definitely awake. This was no dream, but what he was seeing was utterly impossible. The Duck was the size of a Cow, and it was now attempting to get on top of the very bed that Charlie was lying in; as it got onto the bed, the smell of flatulence grew stronger. The Duck's size was such that the bed seemed to scrunch up like paper, as soon as it managed to get itself on top. Charlie felt his legs get squashed, as the feathered horror flapped and squawked in it's attempts to balance itself on the strange Human contraption. Eventually, it righted itself and began to waddle towards the terrified Charlie who could do nothing but lie there in a cesspit of moist sweat. The Duck thrust it's beak towards Charlie's face, and liquid dribbled onto the forehead of the aghast man, causing him to almost throw up in utter revulsion. Any second now, and it seemed as if the colossal bird would take an equally large chunk out of the petrified human who could only stare at it in unbridled horror; Charlie tried to scream but only the merest pathetic croak emerged from his throat. Several seconds later, and he fainted into sweet unconsciousness.

When Charlie awoke, the sun was streaming in through the windows. It was only now that he realised there were no curtains. The smell had gone, and there was no sign of the huge Duck. Hurriedly dressing himself with shaking and fumbling fingers, Charlie almost fell down the stairs in his haste to get away. Of the Landlord and the barmaid, there was no sign and the whole place looked as if it hadn't been used in a month. Charlie fled out of the main door, which was thankfully unlocked, and into his car; revving the engine as fast as he could, he drove off without looking back. If he had, he would have seen the creaking sign hanging outside the Inn now had a `name' where previously there had been none: The Inn.

The Alhambra

The Alhambra
by Jamie Tucknutt

Frank stood out front, checked his watch, almost opening time. He buffed the black peak of his burgundy cap on the sleeve of his burgundy frock coat trimmed with gold piping and then gave a last polish to his shiny name badge, Frank Chettleborough - Commissionaire.

"11 o'clock now would you say Mrs Beaumont?" he asked the lady in the ticket office. She looked at her fob watch and nodded in agreement. Frank rang the big brass bell that hung in the foyer, and had done for as long as anyone could remember. It was as shiny as his own name badge as he polished it every day, and was engraved 'The Alhambra', the finest cinema in town. In Frank's (albeit slightly biased) opinion.

"That should wake Phil up and remind him to load the reel. We don't want a repeat of last week's fiasco when he shone the light from an empty projector onto the screen for a good few minutes before realising the Arthur Askey film was still in the tin."

"Quite," agreed Mrs Beaumont, a touch haughtily as befits a ticket office manageress and unofficial cinema disciplinarian. Many a rowdy child, and indeed adult, had been quietened and threatened with fear of ejection from the premises by nothing more than one of her withering glances or a raised eyebrow. Her facial gestures could speak volumes without uttering a single word. "And I hope Daphne has plenty of ice creams in her tray. The radio said it's going to be a warm day today and they're sure to sell out quickly. Her mind seems elsewhere these days. I think she spends too much time with those Americans."

"Oh Mrs Beaumont," chided Frank, "I'm sure she's sensible enough and is just fine. The young are very different these days." Mrs Beaumont merely wrinkled her nose to register disapproval.

Frank walked out onto the pavement in front of the main door ready to greet the customers. Though, he had to be honest, there certainly weren't as many these days. Still it was a Western today and they usually brought a few extras in."

"That bleedin' freezer's on the blink again," a flustered Daphne announced as she entered the foyer, "over 'alf of me choc ices 'as melted. I think there's only two dozen left."

"I'll take a look at the freezer after the film. I think two dozen will be more than enough though Daphne, full houses seem to be a thing of the past these days. Mrs Beaumont and I were just saying that if it wasn't for the regulars, we'd be struggling. New customers are hard to come by, for obvious reasons."

"Two choc ices please Miss," said a young lad in a cowboy outfit to Daphne, as his similarly dressed friend purchased their tickets for the matinee. They then excitedly made for the auditorium.

“Erm, Frank,” said Mrs Beaumont, peering over her spectacles, “I think we may be about to get a new customer.”
“Really”
“Yes, there’s an old gentleman over the road beside Mrs Gilloway’s dressmaking shop looking very intently this way. Maybe he’s a big Western fan.”
“Oh yes. He is looking very interested, isn’t he? Well spotted Mrs Beaumont. Here he comes.”
Sure enough, an elderly gentleman was crossing the road in the direction of the cinema, a bewildered look on his face. “Mr Chettleborough?’ he asked Frank, then turned to the ticket office, “and Mrs Beaumont? Daphne? What are you doing here?”
“Sorry sir,” replied Frank, “do we know you?”
“Yes, well, er, or rather you did. You may not remember me though. I’m Bert Cooper. Jimmy Cooper’s younger brother.”
Out of the man’s eyeline, Daphne pointed to her temple with a circular motion, “Don’t you mean Jimmy’s grandad or uncle?”
“No. He’s my older brother. Or was.”
“He’s a good lad is Jimmy,” said Frank trying to placate the obviously dotty old man and be a calm voice of reason, “where is he now Bert?”
“Why he’s dead Mr Chettleborough. He was killed in the War.”
“Excuse me,” interrupted Mrs Beaumont, “but I don't find that sort of thing at all funny sir.”
“I’m not trying to be funny,” insisted an increasingly confused looking Bert, “something is very wrong here. Those two boys who just bought a choc ice from Daphne were Fred Whittle and Billy Mason. Two of my classmates at school. They were killed when this place was hit by a Doodlebug. You all were. It was during a cowboy film and I only missed it because I was ill that day. That’s why it’s a memorial park now. You kept going back into the burning building Mr Chettleborough to save the people and it collapsed on you. Look,’ and he pointed behind Frank, Daphne and Mrs Beaumont.
The cinema wasn't there anymore. It was a beautiful little park with lawns and flowerbeds in full bloom. Mothers watched their children playing and people simply enjoying the sun sat reading on their mobile phones. A standing stone marked the centre and Frank read the bronze plaque upon it:

Alhambra Memorial Park
Dedicated to the 97 people who
lost their lives in the Alhambra Cinema
during a German bombing raid
9th September 1944
RIP

The Lepers of Pluto

THE LEPERS OF PLUTO
BY
DAVID BRILLIANCE

The space cruiser StarDart touched down on the planet surface, and several minutes after the retro rockets had ceased their ear-splitting shriek, the hydraulic door on the craft's gleaming silver side hissed open, and a space-suited figure walked out, followed by three more. After examining a small device in it's hand, the figure removed the helmet to reveal the features of a very attractive woman: Lydia Tront was 27 years old, and was the Commander of the StarDart's current mission - which was basically to survey new and unexplored worlds in the Certes cluster. She and her three-man crew had been at it for over a month now, and boredom was beginning to set in; not helped by the fact the new and unexplored worlds the group had encountered thus far had been routine at best.

Lydia turned to one of the suited figures by her side; the helmet had also been removed to reveal the face of Larry Inglestadt, a burly 45 year-old from Chicago who's face had more lines and creases than a 12-foot high pile of unlaundered washing. Larry sniffed the air and nodded "Smells ok to me. We can ditch the suits and helmets anyway". Lydia nodded, touched a switch of the side of her uniform and the entire ensemble vanished with just a click, miniaturised and folded away in a small pouch on the side of the clothes she was wearing underneath the metallic suit. The other two members of the crew had likewise ditched their space suits, and were seen in the formal tight-fitting green and black lycra jumpsuits common to the space service in the year 2340.

Aside from Tront and Inglestadt, the other two crewmembers were in their 20s; Michael Forward, a brash young man with ambition, and Diana Bentley, an attractive blonde who was a bit on the quiet side. Lydia turned to look at the landscape they had arrived in on this latest world - the vista was beautiful; it was a large forest glade with bright sunshine beaming down. The air smelt like wine mixed with honey, and there was a very slight breeze in what was otherwise an agreeably warm day. The whole area seemed like a day in early Summer back on Earth. The trees looked no different to the ones on Earth, the grass underfoot was green, and dotted about were some beautiful plants and flowers of various shapes and colours.

"Right" said Lydia, "let's do our usual reconnaissance and meet back here in about twenty minutes. Fan out!". The others nodded, and they all headed off in different directions. As Lydia walked along, she felt a feeling of incredible peace and calm. The whole area was so tranquil and still. After fifteen minutes walking, she had encountered nothing in the way of animal life, and the wooded area beside which the ship had landed seemed to go on for miles; trees, sunlight, flowers.. That was all this world seemed to offer, and yet.. She would gladly settle down and stake a claim to stay here. Lydia turned around and started to walk back the way she had come. After ten minutes, the serene peace and stillness was shattered briefly by a sudden scream. It was Bentley! Lydia started to run, and came panting to a dead stop in time to see the shattered corpse of the youngest and most inoffensive member of the crew laid on the grass and earth, blood spattered on the ground from what remained of the young girl's head.

"I knew it! I knew it was too good to be true!" thought Lydia bitterly. She bent down and almost tenderly touched the body of the deceased girl, while at the same time keeping a wary eye on her surroundings. From the look of it, Diana Bentley had been killed from close range fire by a laser pistol aimed directly at her head. As Lydia pondered, Inglestadt came crashing into the blood-soaked foliage, a look of utter shock on his face when he observed the remains of his colleague. "What the fuk happened here?" he demanded. Lydia winced slightly; she came from a very well-off family unit and wasn't used to the profanities which were still very much in use by some classes in this time period. She stood up and looked Inglestadt straight in the eye: "I don't know. But before we leave this planet, I will". Lydia sighed deeply, then asked "Have you seen Forward?". Inglestadt shook his head, muttering "We'd better find him, just in case".

After twenty minutes of walking through the same sunny and tranquil environment, the pair eventually caught sight of their crewmate. He was lounging against a tree, bare-footed and casually sucking a long blade of grass in his mouth. He had a slightly simple and dazed grin on his face, a look that didn't alter as he turned at the sound of his two grim-faced superiors striding towards him. "Forward!" barked the older man, "at attention!". The younger man merely looked at him. Lydia came up and repeated the order given by Inglestadt but in s lightly milder tone. This too produced no reaction in the young man, other than a slightly sleazy and suggestive grin. "What can I do for you.. Maaam" he drawled with a suggestive wink that took his commanding officer aback with a start. Lydia looked at Inglestadt, then back to Forward; "Forward, we're leaving this area. Bentley's dead, been shot by a laser. Have you seen anyone or anything while you've been here?".

Forward looked slightly surprised but if he cared in the slightest about the fate of Diana Bentley, it didn't show at all. Instead he turned to both of the others and said in the same dozy drawl "I ain't going nowhere, maam. I'm staying here in this city. Too much to see and do here. Just having me a rest for a few minutes, then I'm gonna check out that casino and bar over the street there, maybe that anti-gravity theatre too". Lydia looked at Forward as if he was insane. "Casino and bar? Forward, we're in the middle of a wood on an unknown planet, and one of the crew has been murdered!". Forward merely grinned at her. Inglestadt balled his fists and moved closer to the young man, snarling in a quietly menacing tone "Listen Mister. When your commanding officer orders you to do something, you do it. Now, put your fukking boots on and follow us, or you'll be facing a court martial when we return to Earth".

Forward just looked at him, grinned and said in a mocking tone "Now, don't you and this sexy little lady here worry none mister. We'll get ourselves a drink, then maybe see a show eh? Got all the time in the world here, and..". Forward never completed the sentence, as the other man punched him right in the solar plexus, causing Forward to double over in pain. Gasping for breath, he straightened up, then without a word aimed a roundhouse blow at Inglestadt's head. The blow missed, as the other ducked but soon the two men were scuffling and rolling around on the grassy earth. Lydia took her blaster from the pouch she was wearing, and fired at the tree nearest the two men. They ignored it, and continued their brawl. Lydia quickly bent down to wrap her hands around the face of the younger man who had gotten on top of the older, and pulled his face backwards, hoping to get him to release his grip on the other. Instead, Forward elbowed her in the ribs, causing Lydia to wheeze in sudden shock and almost fall backwards.

What happened next caused Lydia to almost scream - the two men simultaneously reached for their blasters, the younger man shrieking "I ain't never gonna leave this city!", then they both fired at the same time. The light from the blast caused Lydia to stumble backwards, squeezing her eyes tightly, as a sudden acrid stench of blood and burnt flesh assailed her nostrils. When she eventually managed to open her eyes, she almost gagged at the sight of what was left of the two men.

The next hour was spent in a slight state of shock; Lydia sat and looked at the remains of her crewmates, as the sunlight continued to pour down on her through the treetops. The reverie was broken by the sound of movement from the left, which suddenly had Lydia on her feet, her mind restored to the duty and responsibility mode which she had carried within her for so many years now. As Lydia looked, she could see two.. No, three. Or was it four, or five? No, six, definitely six, figures shambling towards her. They appeared to be a mix of men and women, dressed in tattered rags and with looks of utter misery and pain on their faces. With a sudden thrill of horror, Lydia saw that their skin was covered with leprous multi-coloured blotches..

Lydia remembered. She remembered the early days of space colonisation. One of the first Earth colonies to be established had been on Mars in the year 2245, followed by other worlds in the Solar System. One of the last to be colonised by Humans was Pluto. Everything had seemed to be fine at first, as fine as it had been on the other colonies. But then, the Pluto colonists had found themselves facing a crisis; a disease had blighted the colony, which resulted in symptoms very like leprosy on Earth but much worse; the infected victims had pleaded for death, as they suffered indescribable pain, accompanied by a gradual covering of the entire skin surface by the blotches. Eventually, the final stages had seen the ravaged victims experiencing unbearable agony, followed by madness and death. Earth had done it's best to try to find a cure for the disease, but to no avail. The Pluto colonists were left to die the worst death imaginable, while Earth and it's other colonies continued, attempting to suppress from their thoughts the terrible fate that had befallen their fellow Humans. Lydia had grown up with the stories of the Pluto virus and how it's victims had begged for death, as they proceeded to be covered by the blotches.. As a child, Lydia had spent many hours frantically checking her own skin for signs of the disease; her mother had soothingly reassured her that the virus was confined to Pluto and that she and everyone else on Earth would be safe. Safe…

Lydia's thoughts were interrupted with a scream of utter horror.. She realised that the scream was coming from her own lips. One of the lepers had reached her and grabbed her in an embrace, while one of the others was running his flaky and pus-soaked fingers all over her face and hair. Lydia was almost sick with revulsion; the others were tearing at her clothing, attempting to pull the jumpsuit down. Lydia struggled violently, kicking out at the nearest figure. The kick landed squarely in the wretched fellow's groin, but he shrugged it off, pushing his face close to hers. Tears brimmed from her eyes, as she fought to escape. For one terrible moment, she was forced to look directly into the face of the nearest leper: it seemed an ancient face, teeth missing in a twisted mouth that utterly reeked. Lydia screamed, a long and harrowing scream that grew louder as she caught sight of her own arm and saw that she too was now infected. Nothing ahead but a horrific, painful and lingering death. In agony and madness.. Lydia staggered away from the swaying figures who looked at her with horrible rictus grins. They seemed to be exulting in the fact that she too was condemned to the same unbearable fate.. Lydia reached for the blaster in her pouch, took it out and placing the nozzle in her mouth, fired.

The forest was quiet and still once again, no signs of life, no sounds, no movement. No movement, save for the swaying in a very slight breeze of some of the beautiful and brightly coloured plants that dotted the area. One of the plants seemed to turn and almost look at the other, which also seemed to turn and look slightly. If any Human being had been there, and had been able to understand the telepathic message exchanged between the two plants, they would have heard something that could be passably translated to Earth English as “The intruders have been disposed of once again. Once again, we are alone and at peace. Let all who invade our world be disposed of in the same way”. As I say, this is only a rough translation but the end result remains the same.

The Missing Link

The Missing Link
by Jamie Tucknutt

Well hello again readers, back for more adventures with Wellington Jones and his scrapes, japes and derring-do in the service of Her Majesty Queen Victoria and the British Empire? You may recall how Wellington and Nightingale (who, incidentally is now his wife) halted the evil Mandrake's wicked plot to blow up Brunel's Cross Channel bridge whilst Her Majesty was on the maiden train journey from London to Paris as part of the grand opening. Much has happened in the last few years, poor Brunel is no longer with us (RIP Izzy) and Nightingale is pregnant with their first child so must unfortunately sit out most of this current adventure we are about to come to. Not totally though! Its impossible to even imagine Nightingale staying out of the action. Just this time she's playing a bit more of a cerebral role and a bit less of the martial arts and crack pistol shooting prowess. Anyway, on with the tale.

There were Nightingale and Wellington in their Pimlico townhouse, just about to sit down to dinner when there was an urgent, if not frantic, knocking on the door.
"I'll bet a pound to a penny that's one of the messengers,"said Wellington who, much like Sherlock Holmes, has a retinue of streetwise youngsters keeping him abreast of all of the latest goings on. Nightingale, quick as ever, was already of the same opinion and replied, "I'll get your guns and sword cane while you answer the door. Give me a shout if you need me to divert the hot water."
The Jones's you see, have a high-speed, steam-powered dirigible parked in a rooftop garage and ready to go at a moment's notice. To speed things up even more, and hopefully catch the bad guy in the act, Wellington had added a diverter valve to their domestic hot water supply. This allowed them to fill the dirigible's boiler with pre-heated water this cutting about ten minutes off the time they can leave.
It was indeed one of Wellington's messengers, the 24 hour rolling news service of their day. Nothing and no one made a move in the dark streets and alleyways of a gaslit, night time London without them knowing. This particular messenger was a young lad called Tom.
"Evenin' Mr Jones, you're needed at once Sir. The Crown Jewels 'ave been nicked an' there's murders at The Tower."
"Murders?"
"Yes sir, two Beefeaters killed by the robbers an' the Peelers say it's queer old job."
"Thanks Tom," said Wellington, his mind already going into high gear. He gave the lad a shilling, which of course was gratefully accepted. "Nightingale, I

shan't be needing any weapons nor the dirigible. There'll be no action tonight. But I'm afraid the Crown Jewels have been stolen."

So Wellington found himself on a rainy evening speaking to detectives and the pathologist over the bodies of the two slain Beefeaters.
"Hmm," said Wellington examining the first one, "his head isn't quite turned right through the full 360 degrees, but near enough. I'm guessing cause of death was a broken neck?"
"Indeed," replied the pathologist, "and from what we can gather due to the make up of the scene, this other poor chap must have gone to his stricken comrade's aid and was himself slammed backwards into this wall."
"By a getaway horse or vehicle?"
No. And this is where the mystery deepens. It appears he was struck a blow in the chest, I can confirm a broken sternum and several ribs. His cause of death was a massive head trauma on impact with the wall. Thing is, the blow seems to have a been a punch. Look at this mark." With that he opened the Beefeater's tunic to show Wellington a distinctly fist-shaped bruise in the centre of the victim's chest."
Wellington measured his fist against it, "Somewhat smaller than my own. But it would be impossible for anyone to generate sufficient power in a punch to propel this man against the wall with such force, let alone someone as small as our assailant."
"I should think so," replied the pathologist, "I doubt even Gypsy Gem Mace could punch that hard. Oh, and our plucky Beefeater here did manage to grab a handful of hair, at least I think it's hair, from our robber/murderer. He had this clamped in his right hand when the constables first arrived." The pathologist handed over a thick tuft of coarse, reddish-brown hair. Wellington and Nightingale examined it closely then looked at each other quizzically.
"I see what you mean," said Nightingale, "it is almost too rough to be human hair. But it has to be doesn't it? Unless he grabbed it off some animal such as a horse the robber used to make good his escape. But it doesn't seem thick enough to be equine."
Wellington thought for a second or two then announced, "I know the very chap who can help us. Tomorrow morning I'll pay a visit to Mr Charles Darwin."

Next morning Wellington marched purposefully across the marble floor of the grand foyer to the Natural History Museum, for a librarian he had a remarkably military air and gait. Normally this was one of his favourite London haunts, only this time he was on very important business. Nationally important business.
"What ho Reggie, ready for another influx of inquisitive visitors?" He asked cheerily of Reginald Baxter, long time janitor at the museum.

"Mornin' Mr Jones sir. Yes sir, h'always ready to h'educate the masses we are. Though to me honest Mr Jones, I'd sooner 'ave 'ad the day orf today. Feelin' me age in these old bones this mornin' I am."
"Sorry to here that Reggie, probably this damp weather. Still, at least your bones aren't quite as old as Dippy's here!" Wellington joked, indicating the huge diplodocus skeleton under which they were standing.
"Ha ha, not quite Mr Jones, not quite," Reggie laughed, stroking his beard, "no, he's 150,000,024 years old is the big fella 'ere."
"I say," said Wellington somewhat impressed, "that's very precise ageing there Reggie. I knew you blokes at the museum were good, but I didn't realise you were that good."
"Pretty simple really Mr Jones. I been working 'ere 24 years and on my first day I was told 'e was 150,000,000 years old. So i just adds on the years as I goes."
"Hmm, erm, yes. Good idea Reggie," said Wellington with his famous diplomacy, "is Charles Darwin in at the moment?"
"Yes sir, Mr Darwin is up in his study looking at some h'exotic birds h'eggs."
"Good, I've a devil of a puzzle for him."
'I knew you was on something of a mission Mr Jones. Reggie, I says to meself, there's a man on a mission. Probably a top secret one anorl, being as its Mr Jones I shouldn't wonder. 'Ere, its not to do with the Crown Jewels ball is it? Cor! I bet it is," said Reggie excitedly and secretly pleased to have come up with a deduction of his own.
"No flies on you Reggie," said Wellington. He then tapped his nose and leant in towards Reggie secretively, showing him something he had taken out of his coat pocket, "since the two poor Beefeaters were killed in the raid andwe've no other witnesses, this is the only clue. A tuft of hair taken from one of said Beefeaters' grasp, no doubt as the sterling chap fought to protect the jewels. Very coarse hair. Damned tough stuff it is too. Senior Home Office Pathologist, no less, has categorically stated it is neaither human nor animal. At least to the best of his and his teams knowledge and expertise."
"Ooh, that is a puzzle an' 'arf Mr Jones that is. Mr Charles Darwin, brilliant as 'e is, will 'ave 'is work cut out. But 'ere's my opinion sir, for what its worth. Looks to me like one of them rangy tangies."
"Sorry, a what?"
"Rangy tangy sir. Great big gingery-brown thing, one o' then great h'apes what lives in Borneo and Sumatra. We've got a stuffed one of 'em upstairs sir on display in the primates section. You ought to take a look at it sir."
"Oh, an orang-utan. Yes, thanks Reggie, I might just take your advice," Wellington said, only this time as well as displaying his diplomacy a little, he was also thinking that old Reggie might not be too far off the mark here, "anyway, toodle pip Reggie, must catch Mr Darwin first."

"Right you are sir," replied Reggie doffing his cap respectfully, "always 'appy to 'elp."

Wellington climbed the stairs to the top floor and knocked on the door of the study of one of the foremost minds in the Empire. If anyone could get to the bottom of this conundrum, then surely it was Charles Darwin he thought.
"Come in."
The study was exactly had imagined it would be. Dimly lit by just a couple of reading lamps, every square inch of wall was taken up with fully laden bookcases. A huge, dark oak desk had papers, books, charts and drawings strewn across it. Darwin himself was stood at a large table examining birds eggs under a bright lamp and making notes. Wellington introduced himself and explained the purpose of his visit emphasising how this tuft of unidentified hair possibly held the clue to the stealing of the Crown Jewels. Darwin took the hair between his thumb and forefinger, gently rolling it to feel the texture. He sniffed it a few times, his brow furrowing. He then gave Wellington a very odd look as he passed him to examine the hair under his microscope.
After a couple of minutes examination, and another five or ten checking in one of his books, Darwin looked up, "Well, I know this wouldn't be a practical joke given the gravity of the situation. So my only honest answer as to the origin of the species this hair belongs to is this, it is primate but neither human nor ape. Or, if you prefer, it is both human and ape in that it shares a unique collection of similarities with the two of them. You would appear to have discovered the missing link Mr Jones!"
"In that case Mr Darwin," laughed Wellington, "it is my turn to state that only the gravity of the situation prevents me from taking that as a practical joke. And you are quite sure that it isn't any species you have encountered before?"
"I'm certain Mr Jones. It is undoubtedly on the same evolutionary ladder as us humans, but is unlike any step that we have physical evidence of so far. I'd be most interested in seeing this creature and also meeting the person who both found it and is now controlling it. There simply has to be a trainer of sorts involved who has exploited this creature's superior strength and agility for his own gain in this despicable murder/theft."
"Hmm, then I also foresee a problem for our best legal minds if and when we catch the beast."
"You mean does our judicial system have the flexibility to prosecute something that is, yet isn't human?"
"Quite so Mr Darwin. We don't want to be bracketed with the folk of Hartlepool who hanged the monkey thinking it was a French spy do we?"
"Do you know I always thought that was just a local myth? Ha, well I never."
"No, apparently not. Anyway, I've taken up enough of your precious time. Thank you for your help an I shall bid you good day sir."

"Good bye Mr Jones. Do keep me informed of your progress, I would so like to study this creature when it's caught. Dead or alive."

"Oh, the missing link," said Nightingale excitedly, clapping her hands in delight, "Wellington that's brilliant. Maybe now Mr Darwin's doubters will hold their tongues still. What do you suppose he looks like? What sort of intelligence level will he have? Why did he steal the Crown Jewels? And is he a he?"
"Slow down, slow down!" laughed Wellington, "about the only one of those questions I can answer is why he stole the Crown Jewels. Mr Darwin feels that there must be an owner, trainer, call it what you will, in the background."
"Aah, some devious criminal mastermind? Find him and you'll find the creature. And vice versa of course."
"I was thinking along those lines myself. Clearly this creature has been captured in the wild by an explorer/adventurer type."
"Meaning?"
"Meaning, if we assume the level of training required to get it to break into the Tower and steal the Crown Jewels would take what, say six months? Then maybe if we study who has been where and when in about the last eighteen months, we can possibly narrow down the list of suspects."
"Good thinking Wellington. Presumably it would need to be a fairly large, and very well-financed operation, to capture, keep and train the creature. Therefore we can leave out the University study expeditions, loners and amateur mountaineering groups. Ooh, I just thought. What if there are more than one of these creatures?"
"Now that is something I hadn't thought of. Bloomin' 'eck, imagine if there's an army of them.
Suddenly an almighty crash that Nightingale and Wellington felt as much as heard, reverberated throughout the house.
"That came from the roof," shouted Wellington and he set off at full pelt up the stairs, Nightingale in close attendance. Being several months pregnant was no barrier to her getting involved in a mystery. They both hurtled up to the roof top terrace with its mini hangar for parking the dirigible not to mention a splendid view over all of London. Not that they had time to admire it, at that moment the aforementioned dirigible was being flown away by thieves. Luckily a couple of mooring ropes were swinging loose, Nightingale and Wellington ran to the edge of the roof and with a mighty leap caught hold of one each. Precariously they clung on over a hundred feet above the cobbled streets below. Wellington knew that to even attempt to admonish his wife for such a risky undertaking was futile.
Instead he just rolled his eyes and asked, "Have you given any thought to a name for the baby?"

"I haven't to be honest," she laughed, "though much more of this swinging around and I think it'll be Tarzan if it's a boy!" Just then, shots rang out from the basket some thirty feet above their heads. Nightingale reached for the two shot Derringer pistol from her ankle holster and returned fire. She gripped the rope between her crossed legs to keep her steady as she re-loaded. While his wife was keeping the heads of the thieves down with her covering fire, Wellington climbed up the rope as fast as he could.
"Good shot dear," he said as a body fell past him from the basket, one of Nightingale's bullets in his head.
"Thank you," she replied, then quickly said with undisguised disgust, "Wellington. That fellow is trying to cut your rope. Hey! That's not fair."
Wellington shimmied up to the edge of the basket just as his rope gave way. To save himself from falling he managed to grab the wrist of the man who had done the cutting. The chap dropped his knife and cried out in alarm. The basket swayed wildly as someone came to the thief's aid and grabbed one of Wellington's arms in turn. He couldn't see over the edge of the basket at whoever held him but it was a very strong grip and a very hairy hand. Wellington swung a leg and managed to hook it over and into the basket, he quickly brought the other one over and so was stood facing his two opponents. One was your standard thief, average height, average build etc. But the other. Well, he was naked, covered in thick hair, damned ugly and very smelly to boot. A three man tussle ensued, each trying to extricate himself from the other. Such was the movement of the basket, not to mention Wellington being outnumbered and outgunned, he took a quick look to ensure they were still over the river then decided on a tactical withdrawal by leaping out and taking the other two with him.
"Wellington, where on earth are you going?" shouted Nightingale as a bundle of bodies fell past her. Feeling that her husband might need some help, and the dirigible was insured anyway, she also let go of the rope and splashed down in the Thames a couple of seconds after them. Wellington had the human thief firmly in his grasp, but the ape-man was a few yards away and flailing his arms wildly in a panic-stricken, but seemingly futile attempt to stay afloat.
"Apes can't swim," shouted Nightingale and with a few long, powerful strokes she was behind the creature. She lifted his head clear of the water and tilted it back to enable her to take him ashore to safety.
On a sliver of exposed, muddy river bank, Nightingale carefully sat the creature up and took a step or two away from him. She was anxious to save his life but was also aware of his strength and power and the fact that he may be non-too friendly. Wellington kept a firm grip on his prisoner and said, "Very carefully Nightingale. No sudden movements in case we spook the chap." They need not have worried. Despite the creature's strength and presumed ferocity, he stood as meek as a lamb, his eyes never leaving Nightingale. Whether or not this was

due to her just saving his life, they were unsure. But one thing was certain, he looked upon her with a respectful gaze and when she motioned for him to stand, he did so but wouldn't move another muscle until she beckoned for him to walk towards them.
By now an army of police had arrived and some took Wellington's prisoner from him and put him in handcuffs.
"We'll be taking these chaps direct to Scotland Yard Mr Jones," said a Sergeant, "I've been instructed to ask you to accompany us as well Sir, to aid in the questioning."
The creature however, was unsettled by such a gathering of men around him and bared his teeth menacingly. He let out a deep, rumbling growl as a constable approached him causing the poor fellow to stop dead in his tracks, his knees virtually knocking.
"Allow me," said Nightingale stepping forward and taking the handcuffs. With that she gently reassured to nervous beast that it was fine and he allowed her to place the restraints on his wrists.

A couple of hours later, in the depths of the highest security police cells in the land, several floors underground at Scotland Yard, the captured thief has received a fairly rigorous and physical 'questioning' 19th Century-style. That, and that the fact that as he was now linked to the creature/theft/murders it would be the gallows for him, meant he confessed to pretty much everything he'd done and was continuing to sing like the proverbial canary. His name was Samuel Hewitt, from Virginia US of A, and he worked for a good ol' Southern boy, millionaire rancher Rufus G. Hornswaggler III. It was Hornswaggler who had financed/led the expedition to deepest, darkest Africa where the creature had been found. A whole tribe of them in fact.
Hewitt said, "They all ran off at first sight of us, men, women and children. Some on two legs, some on all fours. They was far too quick and wily for us to catch. The only reason we got that fine specimen was on account of his lady being with child. Once we grabbed her, he came along as quiet as good little choir boy."
Wellington could not have been more disgusted at such loathsome tactics and downright foul play. He raged, "So you mean to tell me that this poor creature, who clearly has no concept of where on earth he is or what he is doing here, has been coerced into becoming a thief and murderer due to his pregnant wife being held hostage and all for one man's greed?"
"Yup, that pretty much neatly sums it up," Hewitt answered, "you see Hornswaggler badly needs the money from the sale of the Crown Jewels. The Confederates are taking a mighty beating in the Civil War back home, and he's set his mind on funding their revival. See, he hates the North and wants to keep his slaves."

Wellington's keen brain was working fast, "Is he off back to America with the jewels now?"
"I don't think so. He'll want the creature too. Sees himself as a showman and impressario. He wants to exhibit them around the country, maybe even up into Canada. Even had an idea to go back to Africa, round up the whole tribe and train the menfolk as his personal army."
"So you'd say he's desperate to get the creature back before he leaves?"
"Reckon so. He's got plenty men and plenty guns to pull it off too."
"We'll see about that," said Wellington, formulating a plan, "Sgt Athelstone."
"Yes sir," answered a barrel chested copper with a thick red beard.
"I'm going to need about a dozen of your best men. Handy in a scrap and good pistol shots too."
"No problem sir, I know the very chaps."
"Good, I think we can set a trap for this Hornswaggler fellow, the thoroughly dislikable blighter that he is."
The plan, based on Hewitt's information and Wellington's own intuition about Hornswaggler's greed and personality traits, was relatively simple in its make up. A supposed public viewing of the creature, with an accompanying lecture by Charles Darwin (with his permission of course) was to take place at the Natural History Museum. Newspapers, posters, printed flyers, even the town criers from various boroughs, all advertised this for two days hence. The trap was to be the fact that the tickets would already be 'sold out' to all enquiries by members of the public. The audience was to be made up of policemen, with further constables stationed throughout the museum as visitors, curators etc. Wellington believed that Hornswaggler would feel this to be his best opportunity, and softest target, to snatch the creature.
Every newspaper that evening and the next morning proclaimed 'Come And See The Missing Link' with details and accompanying drawings (of varying quality and accuracy). Some newspapers described him as being "Darwin's Pet'. While one of the more creationist-leaning ones said he was "Darwin's Cousin' and carried beside the article a caricature of Darwin and an apeman bearing a striking resemblance with both of them eating a banana. Friday afternoon at 2pm in the Main Hall of the museum was the place to be f you wished to see the previously best kept secret of the natural world. The trap was set.

Friday morning at Scotland Yard saw an inspection parade like never before. A dozen of the biggest, toughest-looking police constables London had to offer was assembled. All of them dressed in their finest and trying to appear like learned members of the public attending a Charles Darwin lecture. Sgt Athelstone explained to them one last time the outline of the plan. Every man knew his role. Wellington ensured everyone had a good supply of ammunition,

he knew the Americans loved their guns and would therefore be prepared for a battle.
Nightingale took one look at the whole proceedings and said simply, "This won't work Wellington.'
"And why not?" he asked, a little perplexed. It wasn't like him not see any potential glitch in a plan.
"Just look. How realistic an audience does this seem?"
"Granted they're a bit on the brawny side. And with the odd broken nose or cauliflower ear they resemble a gathering of prize fighters. But they've all dressed well and when they're spread around the place it won't look as obvious."
"I think you're missing my point Wellington. What makes these so different from a usual museum crowd?"
After a second or two of study, the penny, and Wellington's face, dropped, "of course," he exclaimed, slapping himself on the forehead, "No women. My goodness me where can we get enough women to do this at such short notice?"
Sgt Athelstone, after overhearing the conversation, felt he had the answer, "Pardon me Mr Jones sir. But we've still got several in the cells from last night's arrests."
"I say sergeant, you might just have the eleventh-hour solution there."
Athelstone walked to a desk and returned with a big, leather bound custody log, "Here we are sir. Eight prostitutes, five pickpockets, four burglars and an actress who was drunk and disorderly. There's also two ladies who were fighting in a pub but they won't do for this task I'm afraid. Faces are a bit scratched and marked up."
"Lead on to the cells sergeant," said Wellington with a new spring in his step, "we'd better see if they can help us."
A few hasty interviews later, and after the promise of all charges dropped plus a £5 reward each, Wellington had his dozen. All ready to pose as the wives or sweethearts of the undercover policemen. The actress, hugely embarrassed at her unseemly behaviour and language the previous evening, was applying make up to the ladies and teaching them how to walk and carry themselves so as to blend in to the surroundings without looking out of place.
"Oh my giddy aunt Mr Jones," said Sgt Athelstone, "never in my born days did I expect to be going out on a job like this with women in my crew!"
"Mark my words sergeant, one day our fine police force will have as many women constables as men. And not before time. The best team is always the one that can blend all of the various skills of its players. After all, you wouldn't win a cricket match if your team consisted of eleven wicket-keepers would you?"
"You're right of course. I just hope none of them gets hurt when the bullets start to fly."

"Me too sergeant. Me too."

The last preparation prior to the lecture cum trap was for Nightingale to brief the creature as best she could. Her advanced state of pregnancy clearly struck a chord with him and reminded him of his wife who they were all trying to reunite him with. Through mimes, gestures, motions and rehearsing movements, she felt she had somehow got him to understand what was going to happen and what he himself had to do. That was, to stay close to Darwin as both would be protected by Wellington and Sgt Athelstone when any shooting started. The platform from which Darwin was to give the lecture had a trap door fitted which only needed him to depress a button on the floor and he and the creature would drop to the relative safety of a below floor space.

At 2pm precisely, Darwin's lecture began, "Ladies and gentlemen, please forgive my smugness as I introduce to you definitive proof that my Theory of Evolution is correct," then with a theatrical extension of his arm and lowering of a red velvet curtain, the creature, sat on a stool, came into view, "I give you, The Missing Link." A couple of gasps from the crowd and the looks of astonishment from the ladies present, and the constables who had yet to have seen the creature, almost had Darwin in the frame of mind that he was giving an actual lecture to students. Just as he was about to get into his stride however, all hell broke loose.
Raised voices, then shouting, a scuffle, even gunshots could be heard from just outside the hall. Seconds later the huge oak double doors burst open and the scene quickly changed form lecture theatre to Wild West bar room brawl and shoot-out. Chairs, exhibits, bullets and fists were flying. One constable restrained two of Hornswaggler's men by clubbing them insensible with a tusk he had broken off a nearby woolly mammoth exhibit.
"Darwin, the button," shouted Wellington pointing to the round brass knob on the floor. Darwin stamped on it, but nothing happened.
"It's not working Wellington," he said, then grabbed the creature and they both ducked behind the lectern out of sight.
"Keep your head down then."
"No kidding," replied the 19th Century world's most eminent scientist and thinker who had obviously already deduced that this was his best course of action to take.
Amidst the melee, it was becoming clear that the trap had worked and Hornswaggler and his band of men had been outwitted. The constables were rounding up and handcuffing any thugs that were still standing, with a bit of help from their escorting ladies whose night time occupation meant that they weren't averse to a bit of street-fighting when it was called for. Indeed, several Americans received pokes to the eye, kicks in the shin and knees to the groin.

In sheer desperation, as he could see no other way of avoiding his imminent capture, Hornswaggler grabbed Nightingale by the arm. Ordinarily, she would have given him a lightning quick punch to the throat but he held his Colt 45 revolver to her head in his other hand. The place fell silent, all movement ceased and all eyes were on them both. The last remaining villain and his hostage.
"Get them to free us boss," shouted one of his men as the police dragged him away to custody.
"Sorry guys, no time or space for you all now. I'm afraid it's every man for themselves," Hornswaggler said. Then facing Wellington he offered the obvious ultimatum, "Tell your coppers to let me out of here or your little lady here gets a bullet between the eyes and blood all over her pretty dress."
Wellington looked at Nightingale as first she rolled her eyes at Hornswaggler's pathetic sexism and his belief he was controlling the situation, then she gave a quick flick of her head and he read the signal.
"Lower your guns gentlemen, let him pass," he said.
"I've got a clear shot sir," said an armed copper from behind a stuffed polar bear.
"Thank you Constable," said Wellington, "but no. Lower your weapon."
"Now that's mighty sensible son," gloated Hornswaggler, "you're smart enough to know when you've been b-" In a flash, Nightingale dipped at the knees, grabbed Hornswaggler's wrist in both hands, bent him forwards and turned his arm upwards so the only shot he managed before dropping the gun went harmlessly into the ceiling.
Then, out from the janitor's cupboard nearby came a rampaging Reggie Baxter armed with his zinc mop bucket. He whacked Hornswaggler across the head with it, CLANG! "That's for man 'andlin' Missus Jones." Then, as the portly American fell to the floor, Reggie, in a nod to his bareknuckle boxing days of a misspent youth when he fought under the name of The Bermondsey Bulldog, caught him flush on the jaw with a left hook. "An' that's for bein' 'orrible to old Monkey Face, the rangy tangy."
All that was left was for Sgt Athelstone to apply the handcuffs to a very dazed Crown Jewel thief and load him into the wagon with the rest of his soundly thrashed crew.
Wellington escorted them all back to Scotland Yard, where they were to be questioned. Nightingale meanwhile, treat all of the brave ladies to afternoon tea back at the Jones house as a thank you.

Afterword

The old saying goes that there is honour among thieves, well not among this lot. The threat of the gallows or substantial prison sentences had them all turning on their rotund boss. He'd promised them all fortune and fame if they could pull off this scheme and win the American Civil War. The rope, or a dark, dingy cell in Brixton prison didn't have the same allure. Tongues were loosened, safe houses and further accomplices given up and the creature was at last reunited with his pregnant wife.

Ug and Mrs Ug, as they came to be known due to that being their most used vocalisation, were eventually taken back to their homeland after the birth of their daughter. But not before thousands of well-wishers across the country, on reading the full story in the newspapers, had knitted baby clothes and bonnets for Baby Ug.

If you look closely on your next visit to London at Dippy the Diplodocus's right hind leg, you'll see a couple of bullet holes from the shoot out that occurred there. It came to be known in Metropolitan Police History as the Gunfight at the Natural History Museum.

Oh, and Wellington was right about women police officers in the end. The first female constable was Edith Smith in 1915.

The Weardale Horror

The Weardale Horror
by David Brilliance & Jamie Tucknutt

Chapter One - Komozum (by Jamie Tucknutt)

Komozum was hungry. Not just hungry either, he was full of the anticipation that goes before a kill. A special kill too, a return to one of his favourite hunting grounds, Planet Earth. He was looking forward so much to feeding on that tasty human blood that he was positively salivating from all three of his mouths. Yes, three. For Komozum wasn't just any killer. He was probably the Universe's most prolific and feared shape-shifting, blood-sucking serial killer. With the fastest, most elusive ship, and the ability to travel through both time and/or space, he was uncatchable to police forces across the numerous planets, eras, galaxies and epochs in which he had plied his evil trade.

Komozum didn't have a home planet as such. He'd been born in the explosion of a massive supernova and, with all of the accompanying destructive forces flowing in his veins, he craved chaos, hatred and suffering (as long as he wasn't the one suffering, that is). They appealed to him, they were his home and his comfort zone. Therefore, it seemed natural that he was drawn to Earth in 2022. It was giving off bad vibes in waves which pulsed across the cosmos and were easily picked up by Komozum's antennae. Eleven antennae to be exact which sat upon the vast, shapeless, pulsating blob that was his body. Translucent and with his innards, vital organs and body fluids clearly visible, he was a revolting sight. All of this was carried on eight long, slender hairy legs akin to a giant tarantula. Each leg ended in an incredibly sharp, bony point, just one of the many fearsome features he used to kill when in his natural form. However, as I have said, Komozum was capable of shape-shifting and used this ability to blend in with the inhabitants of whatever planet he happened to be using as his hunting ground.

It wasn't just the thrill of the hunt, the excitement of the kill or the drinking of his slain victim's blood that Komozum found intoxicating and kept him coming back for more. He also absorbed, as if they were carried in the blood themselves, the skills, knowledge and abilities that the victims had possessed at the time of their deaths. This latter feature of his killing meant that Komozum shivered briefly when recalling his last trip to Earth. It had taken him a little while, and a dose of strong medication, to rid himself of the tuberculosis and syphilis he'd inadvertently taken in from the five poor, unfortunate women he had slaughtered in the east end of Victorian London. This had taken the edge of his overall enjoyment of an otherwise highly successful killing spree. He'd really enjoyed himself appearing as a tall gentleman with a top hat and dark cloak. He did love to dress up. It amused him greatly to see that he was recreated by artists in numerous newspapers and given the nickname of Jack the

Ripper. Komozum felt that Earth glamorised its serial killers far more than any other planet and far more than was good for them. Still, he wasn't complaining, he was back for more after all.
As all successful and, therefore, still at large serial killers are, Komozum was cautious. This time he'd miss out London, he'd heard the Jack the Ripper killings were still unsolved so maybe the case was still open, and instead headed north. Remote, rural Weardale in County Durham to be precise. With its dark winter nights and scattered farmhouses, Komozum thought he would be able to get several kills in here before the alarm was raised.
He left his spaceship in the cover of an old quarry and headed across the river into the nearest village, a place called Stanhope. In the main street night, and darkness had fallen. A single building, among its silent neighbours, was emanating music and voices and a glow at each window. Komozum deduced it was a public house, and it certainly seemed to be an improvement from the ones on his visit to 1888 Whitechapel.
Just then, two humans stepped out through the door. Due to their hairy faces, Komozum thought they must be men. From their male-pattern baldness, and especially their dire wardrobe, he calculated them to be mid-50s in Earth years. He felt a little dismayed. Yes they would slake his thirst for blood, and human blood was his favourite tipple, but what possible talents, knowledge or skills could these two nondescript Average Joes possess? He followed at a distance, keeping himself in the shadows and eavesdropped their conversation.
"Where shall we go next David?" asked the taller of the two who required those corrective glass lens held in frames to boost his ailing eyesight, "Grey Bull?'
The one called David nodded agreement then said, "Hang on Jamie, I've just got to go to the cashpoint first." Komoozum watched and waited and they walked along the street past a church yard chatting inanely, so he thought.
Just as Komozum was getting a little bored and thinking he may attack now and be done with it, he suddenly heard them discuss Daleks. One of his sworn enemies. They were talking about a Dalek invasion of earth in 2350AD. Komozum smiled to himself, a repulsive sight with all three mouths contorting and twisting. Wow, he thought, how wrong I was. These two must have experience of space and time travel to know of these things. Maybe they even know of a Dalek weakness. He so longed to add a Dalek to the list of intergalactic species he had killed. Perhaps they will be a worthwhile kill after all. He quickened his pace, all eight bony legs scritching and clicking on the cobbled road.

CHAPTER TWO - HARE TODAY
BY
DAVID BRILLIANCE

The two men walked along the street to the cash point, and after a few minutes, they turned and headed back along the street. Komazum was studying them intently, being no more than six Earth feet away from them but totally unobserved, as he had changed his appearance to blend in with the planet and this particular environment - he didn't know exactly what Earth creature he had `become' but it must have been a familiar sight to the creatures of this world, as the two men took not the slightest notice and continued ambling along the street.

Their course took them past a large stone monument, past several buildings and then to another street. Komazum followed, chuckling to himself gleefully, as he relished the kill to come. The two men were coming within range of another building that had lit windows, and the sounds of... was it `music' or some such foolery? Komazum had encountered this weird phenomenon of harmonics and sounds on several other worlds but he had yet to understand it's purpose; anything that did not involve slaughter, genocide and large amounts of bodily fluid did not interest Komazum.

"I'll get the first round in" said David, fumbling in his pocket for one of the crisp tenners he'd just taken from the whirring cash machine. Jamie and David attracted the attention of the barmaid, and made their orders - a pint of Guinness for Jamie and a pint of Dark Fruit Strongbow for David - then settled back in a pair of comfy seats to continue their conversation about the merits of 1970s DC and Marvel comics, and which was better. Jamie remained a fervent Marvel supporter, having been brought up on the weekly Marvel UK comics (David: "They were just cheap black and white reprints, with new art added and bits of the story missed out") that encompassed everything from Planet of the Apes (Jamie: "I'll concede it wasn't a good idea to reprint the US Killraven stories and change the title to Apeslayer to make the strip fit") to Spider-Man. David, on the other hand, though he too was a Marvel buff preferred DC ("Superman and Batman are the best comic characters ever created - Fact") and the two enjoyed regular verbal jousts as to the pros and cons of both companies, though they did both agree that both DC and Marvel were past their best by 1987.

Their chatter was interrupted by a piercing shriek from one of the patrons, of which there were about eight as it was a relatively quiet Tuesday night. The shriek had come from a young woman who had been surprised by the sudden appearance in the pub of an intruder, but once over her initial surprise was now reaching down to pat a Hare on the head. David noted that the Hare seemed to have a strange look on it's furry face - distaste? Anger? Surely not..

"Ooh! Where'd this character come from?" enthused Jamie, a lover of all forms of animal life. David and Jamie went across to where Stacey Stellfox was holding up the Hare which seemed to be docile enough, and took turns patting the little creature on the head, and both men couldn't help but notice at this point that it seemed to be.. Well, definitely sort of angry, if that was possible in a Hare. However, it didn't attempt to bite or flee from the scene but just sat there in Stacey's arms, as she continued to pat, kiss and stroke the creature, accompanied by the odd stroke slipped in by the two men. "Hey lads!" called out one of the regulars, "you should get a bunch of them and glue them to your heads! You could do with a headful of Hares each!". David and Jamie turned, and laughed. They were respected regulars in the pub, and the cheeky git with a voice that sounded like someone gargling barbed wire was their old friend Denise, also a regular public house patron.

"Well, see you later Hartley" said David, giving the Hare one last pat. He and Jamie walked over to where Denise had appeared, and were just about to sit down near the dartboard when all Hell seemed to break loose. Stacey Stellfox screamed but this time it wasn't a shriek of delighted surprise, but rather a full-on yell of terror! The Hare had wriggled out of her grasp, then seemed to change in a couple of seconds, becoming first an amorphous blob, then a bigger creature with eight legs which now looked female and clad in dark nylon. The upper part of the torso had two massive, pendulous breast-like appendages, and Jamie caught the briefest glimpse of large red eyes adorned with false eyelashes. All this for just a second, before the huge alien creature's newly-acquired feminine clothing and attributes vanished; squatting in the centre of the now deserted pub (the patrons and staff alike had all fled screaming within seconds) was what the two men obviously took to be an alien monster - and one that was hostile.

The two men looked at one another quickly, then as one they grabbed hold of the nearest table and upturned it, intending to use it as a battering ram or at least a shield, as the creature obviously intended to do them harm. The thing chuckled.. "Ah" it uttered through rancid lips "resistance. Futile resistance of course, but that is so much the better! I like to see my victims suffer!". The table lasted for no more than three seconds, disintegrated into fragments, leaving David and Jamie defenceless. As they watched, the thing extended a long globulous antenna from it's body, and aimed it right at the two men. It seemed to gloat in exultation, as it's body rippled with what the men presumed to be laughter. David and Jamie had not a second to react, as a luminous green ray struck them both, leaving only a thin wisp of some vaporous substance and the ghostly after-image of their astonished and unbelieving faces to indicate that they had ever been stood there..

TO BE CONTINUED

Chapter 3 - El Tortuga (by Jamie Tucknutt)

Fear not, our intrepid heroes aren't dead, yet. Komozum has the ability to fire, from one of his many tentacles and appendages, a teleport beam. This allows him to transport potential prey/victims back to his ship quickly and thus avoid public battles in crowded places such as this.
Unfortunately, from Komozum's point of view, he is unable to teleport himself and so must go on foot. All eight of the bony, hairy, disgusting things. As he was in his natural form, and therefore totally repellant if not terrifying to humans, he thought he'd give everyone in the pub one last scare before he departed. He unleashed a blood-curdling scream from all of his mouths, giving a full display of his deadly fangs.
Everyone shrank back in horror except for one drunk bloke who congratulated him on his Jabba the Hutt costume but questioned, "Why the legs? If you looked a bit more closely, you'd see he sort of slithers along. Somewhat slug-like you might say. Hic." Komozum thought of killing him but then calculated there'd be more beer in his system than blood and didn't want to be drink driving his ship later. He left the pub and scurried along the road before disappearing up a cobbled lane leading to the quarry, clip-clopping like a troop of horses.
Meanwhile, back on board Komozum's ship 'El Tortuga', David and Jamie were overjoyed. In the space of a couple of minutes they'd been attacked by a monstrous creature (probably alien, they had concluded), physically teleported and were now in some bizarre type of craft (possibly a spaceship, they thought). Only it felt, well, a bit more organic than anything they had expected.
"I think we've been teleported back to his ship!" David beamed.
"How strange," said Jamie as he tapped the wall next to him then examined it closely, "it's like we're inside a tortoise or turtle shell. Look at the texture, colours, even the pattern of the scutes. This is definitely something like keratin."
Despite the ship being roughly the size of an ambulance, our sci-fi nerds were right on the money. It was Komozum's spaceship, and it was a living creature closely resembling a turtle. In fact, the only ways in which it differed was that it had eight flippers and could fly through space and time! El Tortuga, as Komozum had called her, was controlled (to a certain degree) by a psychic link which existed between the two. But, as any pet owner will tell you, no matter how well-trained you feel your particular animal is, they will always possess that wilful streak. El Tortuga had a tendency to get a little bored when Komozum was off killing and drinking blood and she'd been left to her own devices. She would then wander off looking for a body of water to swim in and perhaps a little food.

The quarry Komozum had landed in was long disused and had been allowed to revert back to a pre-industrial state and was now a nature reserve. It had a wonderful lake full of fish and eels. El Tortuga loved fishing and so, once she had came across the lake, she dived straight in her yellow eyes glowing like underwater lights to cut through the dark and murky depths.
David looked through a completely transparent scute at the front and centre of El Tortuga's shell, directly above her head. "This must be what that thing uses as a windscreen," and he watched in awe at the speed and manoeuvrability of the craft/creature as she caught and consumed one fish after another.
- It is, can I ask who you are?
"Did you hear that?" asked Jamie.
"I'm not sure heard is the word," answered David, "it just sort of appeared in my head."
"Mine too."
- That's because I communicate silently. With thought transference.
"Are you the creature that just zapped us?" asked David.
- No. I'm the creature you are standing in. Komozum 'zapped' you and sent you here, I'm his ship.
- Are you receiving this? Jamie thought to the ship as he attempted telepathic communication for the first time. El Tortuga had received the message but before she could answer…
- El Tortuga, where are you? boomed so loud in the heads of David and Jamie that they were sent sprawling dizzily to the floor clasping their ears.
- I'm swimming, showing David and Jamie the depths of the lake.
- You aren't supposed to befriend the captives, I'm going to kill them.
- Oh no, you're not
- What??
- Jamie showed me pictures of his pet turtle. Video footage as well on his hand held device. She's called Squirtle. He lives in harmony with her, him and his wife buy her presents and play with her in the garden. I think this puts your treatment of me in a whole new light.
- This is neither the time nor the place.
- But you chose the place. You always choose the place. I think it's time things changed a little.
- But, but, I need to kill them. I'm a serial killer. It's what I do.
- Well, not this time. I've promised to take them back to our secret base planet and show them around. They're intrigued now I've told them it's the only flat planet in the entire Universe. [editor's note - yes that's right all you Flat Earth Society. The <u>only</u> flat planet. Earth is a sphere, accept it. Also Covid wasn't caused by 5g and wearing those tin foil hats doesn't actually block anything, it just makes you look even dumber than you are. Now back to the story.]

- Look, I'm sorry I left you alone. That I always leave you alone. But my job isn't very pleasant at times. Now please come back, we can discuss it further when we're off this planet.
- Promise you won't kill them?
- I promise
- If you do, I'll disappear somewhere in space and time and you'll never see me again.
- I said I promise, didn't I? Now come back to where I left you.
- In a short while, this water is lovely and clean. Not like the last time we were on Earth. Remember? London 1888? The Thames was filthy.
Though very angry, Komozum thought he'd bide his time. He had three brains and one of them he used only for pure evil and right now, in the depths of that very brain, he was planning on breaking his promise, killing the two Earthlings and also killing El Tortuga. He couldn't allow that level of disobedience to go unchecked now could he? He'd pick up another ship and train it to his standards fairly quickly. Oh, he could almost taste that human blood.

FINAL CHAPTER - THE BEGINNING
BY
DAVID BRILLIANCE

David and Jamie both turned in unison, as they heard the unmistakeable and smooth hiss of a hydraulic door moving upwards. Komozum was back, and he was not happy. El Tortuga had resurfaced from the lake and had travelled back to the huge gravelly knoll where it had earlier been parked, awaiting the return of it's master and pilot. Komozum looked around the control room as if seeing it for the first time; then his multi-faceted eyes caught sight of the two humans he had intended to use as prey on his home planet.

The two men looked at their captor with mingled disgust, awe and fascination. Komozum's fetid breath hung in the air near their nostrils: "You two are going with me to my home planet" the creature hissed, relatively quietly, "and once there, you will suffer the most exquisite agonies and tortures that even the Assassin Worms of Gleblor could not dream up! You will both beg for the tender mercy of a quick slitting of your throats and explosion of your gizzards.. El Tortuga!" Komozum rapped the last two words sharply, at his sentient vessel. Then all was silence, as Komozum seemed to be communicating entirely by telepathy to his slightly disobedient ship cum pet. Several moments later, the craft lifted off. It seemed that Komozum was heading back to his planet, and the terrible tortures that awaited his two Human captives..

Jamie, unseen by the still Komozum was slowly removing the screw top of a small jar that he had taken from his inside pocket. David whispered "What's that? What are you doing?". Jamie responded in a similar whisper: "Beetroot. I forgot I had it. Judith asked me to get some at the co - op cos she needs it for something she's making tomorrow. I'm thinking it could help us get out of this mess". David thought for several seconds and then his wired SF fan brain clicked into gear. "I see! You're going to pour the juice into the ship's workings and see if it bungs something up!". Jamie nodded "Right! Just like in the 1969 Doctor Who story The Krotons and where the Martians in the 50s War of the Worlds are done in by the common cold.". Not to be outdone, David rejoined with "It's a common trope in SF that ordinary Earth stuff is fatal to aliens, like in the Outer Limits episode Specimen: Unknown, where alien plants are destroyed by rain on Earth. This beetroot juice might just make our alien killing machine's Turtle friend feel a bit uncomfortable. Great idea James!".

Jamie had managed to get the lid off the jar without being detected. He now carefully tilted the jar and poured all the purple vinegar inside into a tube that was connected to a main power grid by the looks of it, and which might as well have had a sign saying SOMETHING VERY IMPORTANT slapped on it. Several minutes later, and green smoke had started to pour out of the nearby conduits; smoke that didn't go unnoticed by the still-ranting master of the craft. Within a few more minutes, the smoke had increased tenfold, the alarm klaxon of the vessel went into overdrive, and the now-straining engines of El Tortuga were as red as the face of the enraged master of the craft, who was screaming commands impotently, whilst brandishing a large, and similarly impotent weapon.

"I think it's worked!" yelled David above the din of the engines, and the general chaos. "Certainly has!" rejoined Jamie, "you could say it's put some fleas into the Turtle's pubes!". Komozum was swept off his hairy feet, as the craft lurched sickeningly from side to side on a course that didn't seem to be taking it into outer space..

The Stanhope Church stood proudly in the moonlight. It was a quarter past midnight by now, and the echoes of the tolling midnight bell had faded along with the footsteps of revellers returning from the various hostelries that the village offered. It was a scene of pure serene calm. Until at precisely 0.18, when a massive space vessel shaped like an Earth Turtle came whizzing through the skies and, with a shattering roar of it's engines proceeded on a haphazard course that finally ended when El Tortuga crashed head-first through the Church's clock tower, sending the huge dial spinning like a giant blue Frisbee onto the cemetery below. By the time the clock face cum Frisbee had ended it's careening course, a dozen or more headstones had been demolished, along with the churchyard wall, the seats outside, and even the large stone monument. El Tortuga then seemed to lose momentum and power at the same time, and dropped like an enormous Turtle-shaped stone through the roof of the building, sending out huge wreathes of noxious smoke. Sounds of shouting, interstellar swearing and muffled bangs and crashes could be heard from inside, as the interior of the wrecked Church lit up like a paedo's face in an untended orphanage.

The first living thing to emerge from the Church's ruined door was David, followed by Jamie. Both were bent over double and wracked with coughing, as the choking fumes forced themselves into their throats. Both men staggered onto the main path leading up to the Church, and then ran for the huge gap where a wall had once been. Komozum shortly emerged from the wreckage of his vessel; or rather, the men thought, what was left of him emerged - the alien had seemingly lost all but two of his legs in the crash, and only a single bloody stump remained of his various tentacled appendages. The stump was oozing a thick mucous liquid of some dark orange variety, and of the missing appendages, there was no sign. Komozum roared when he caught sight of the two humans - the humans who had done what no other beings in the twenty five and a half galaxies had ever dared to do! They had frustrated his plans, and more than once!! Oh, how they would suffer!

Komozum half ran, half hobbled in a ridiculous hopping fashion; Jamie and David would have laughed if they hadn't been fleeing for their lives! The two men grimaced in surprise and pain as a searing beam of ultra-light orange came whizzing over their heads at so close a distance that it threatened to burn off what little hair they had remaining. Jamie turned and yelled "Bastard!" at the pursuing alien monstrosity, as it hopped furiously in the direction of their startled cries.

At this late hour, the streets were empty - empty that is save for a solitary dog walker who was at that moment staring in disbelief at the ruined church, wall and monument, whilst simultaneously waiting for his German Shepherd, Gustav, to finish taking a leak by one of the two wrecked and upturned wooden seats. The dog's leisurely leak was interrupted suddenly, as two balding, middle-aged men came hurtling out of what had been the entrance to the Church, gesticulating wildly and shouting for the dog and it's confused owner to get clear. In the general melee, the dog and it's master ran hell for leather down the front street, while Jamie and David followed, pursued by the screeching horror that was leaving an orange trail in it's wake as it hopped furiously after them, claws flexing, like a demented and sex-crazed kangaroo on a promise.

With a colossal roar, the Turtle-shaped ship inside the wrecked Church exploded in a dazzling burst of purple light. This radiance seemed to spread, and soon not only the remains of El Tortuga but the remnants of the Church, cemetery, streets outside.. In fact, the whole of Stanhope, had vanished..

David and Jamie came to. The sky above their heads was a brilliant and rich blue. Once they had fully recovered, the two men tried to get their bearings. It was a moderate climate, and they were standing in a field. It seemed strangely familiar. Within a few minutes of walking, the pair realised that they were still in Stanhope, but "not the Stanhope we came from" pondered Jamie, stroking his beard thoughtfully. "I see what you mean" replied David. "This isn't the 21st-century" he added, slowly. Somehow, the explosion of the Turtle ship's engines, perhaps combined with the strange alien substance known as beetroot vinegar, had sent the whole of the Weardale village into a time warp. They were now in.. when? 1730? 1865? 2002? It was impossible to tell without further exploration.

They soon realised that certain fragments of El Tortuga had been thrown back into time with them, and had survived the crash relatively unscathed…

This story was passed down from my Grandfather, who told it exactly as the two men told it to him. David and Jamie you see had found themselves in the year 1958, a year just on the cusp of many new technological advances.. Advances that our two heroes were fully aware of and able to exploit via their prior knowledge of what was to come. Within a year, they were both mega-rich and mega-successful, leading the world into a new Golden Age of peace and prosperity. Among their many lasting legacies was the creation of a new drive to explore space in the form of `El Tortuga‘, a space agency that ended up being formed in the year 1970 and which continues to this day.

If you would like to know exactly what happened to David and Jamie next, then keep an eye out for the next book in the series, which will continue their story.

Afterword

Afterword

That's it, you've finished the book now. There's only a couple of pages about the authors and their damned ugly photographs to go, and no-one eve reads those, do they? I mean, yes I like your books, but I'm not really bothered where you lived/studied/hitch-hiked during gap year.
Suffice to say if you have any comments, good or bad, we've both got ridiculous names so we're fairly easy to find on social media and we agreed at our 'editorial meeting' (a chat outside the Co-op really) that we'd both be happy to receive any constructive criticism, praise or downright abuse. Another thing we agreed on was that my story of a superhero called Chodman couldn't make the cut. Basically, he's like Spiderman but fires high-speed jets of liquid poo from his wrists instead of webs. Yes, Steampunk and Solarpunk are fine, but Shitpunk is maybe a step too far. What do you think?

Meet the Authors

David Brilliance was born in the Summer of Love, June 1967, and soon discovered that not only did he hate football, but that he loved science fiction and horror. So while many of his schoolmates all enjoyed watching men kicking a cow's bladder around a field and kissing one another when they scored, David enjoyed reading the delights of many a monster mag or watching TV and films to such an extent that he was soon quoting the TV listings pages of the local newspaper by the age of five. David has worked in various jobs over the years - skillfully avoiding the hairdressing profession that many of those schoolboy football fans ended up in - and currently resides in picturesque Weardale, where he continues writing and describes himself as a `Hopeful Guinea Pig in the Laboratory of Fate'.

Jamie Tucknutt is 55 years old (I know, he looks **much** younger) and he lives in County Durham with his wife Judith and their rescue animals, a dog Peggy, a cat Teabag and Squirtle the Turtle.
They can often be found touring the UK in their bright yellow VW camper. So if you see them, give them a wave. Or a push if it has broken down again.

Printed in Great Britain
by Amazon

22783087R00086